Conno

He wanted h
around him
humour she carried around with her like
sunshine.

And he wanted to touch her. To fill his hands
with her silken mane of hair and run it through
his fingers and lower his mouth to hers and kiss
her until he was dizzy.

And *that* was what was keeping him from
picking up the phone.

Because the woman he was thinking about was
Andie Spencer—his best friend.

Dear Reader:

Welcome to Silhouette Desire — provocative, compelling, contemporary love stories written by and for today's woman. These are stories to treasure.

Each and every Silhouette Desire is a wonderful romance in which the emotional and the sensual go hand in hand. When you open a Desire, you enter a whole new world — a world that has, naturally, a perfect hero just waiting to whisk you away! A Silhouette Desire can be light-hearted or serious, but it will always be satisfying.

We hope you enjoy this Desire today — and will go on to enjoy many more.

Please write to us:

Jane Nicholls
Silhouette Books
PO Box 236
Thornton Road
Croydon
Surrey
CR9 3RU

What Are Friends For?

NAOMI HORTON

*First published in Great Britain in 1995
by Silhouette Books, Eton House, 18-24 Paradise Road,
Richmond, Surrey TW9 1SR*

© Susan Horton 1994

*Silhouette, Silhouette Desire and Colophon are
Trade Marks of Harlequin Enterprises B.V.*

ISBN 0 373 59398 8

22-9501

Made and printed in Great Britain

NAOMI HORTON

was born in northern Alberta, where the winters are long and the libraries far apart. "When I'd run out of books," she says, "I'd simply create my own—entire worlds filled with people, adventure and romance. I guess it's not surprising that I'm still at it!" An engineering technologist, she presently lives in Nanaimo, British Columbia, with her collection of assorted pets.

Other Silhouette Books by Naomi Horton

Silhouette Desire

Dream Builder
River of Dreams
Split Images
Star Light, Star Bright
Lady Liberty
No Walls Between Us
Pure Chemistry
Crossfire
A Dangerous Kind of Man
The Ideal Man
Cat's Play
McAllister's Lady
No Lies Between Us
McConnell's Bride
Chastity's Pirate

Silhouette Sensation

Strangers No More
In Safekeeping
Dangerous Stranger
Born To Be Bad

Silhouette Christmas Stories 1993
"Dreaming of Angels"

One

___

She'd been half expecting the call. But even so, the phone still managed to startle her badly when it finally rang, the sound shrill in the late-night stillness of her bedroom. Andie jerked awake and swore breathlessly, heart pounding with automatic alarm, and blinked into the darkness, wondering what in heaven's name time it was.

Late—she knew that much. He never called unless it was late. In the daylight, he was too sure of himself, too full of that male self-confidence he wore like a cloak to allow himself to be beset by doubts and questions and pain. It was only in the dark, late at night, when his demons would slip free and taunt him from the silences of his mind. And that's when he'd call her.

Andie Spencer, dragon slayer.

She smiled grimly and squinted groggily at the digital clock by her bed. Not this time, hotshot. You can just put those dragons to rest all on your own, because I am *not* coming out there tonight. Not this time. No way. Not at . . . oh, God, four-thirty in the morning. Groaning, she stared at the clock in disbelief. Four-thirty!

Somehow she managed to grab the receiver without knocking over the stack of books teetering on the edge of the table.

"Conn." She dropped back into the soft contours of her pillow, eyes closed, the receiver tucked against her ear.

There was a pause, then a familiar husky male chuckle. "How the hell do you do that, anyway? Know it's me, I mean."

"Who else calls me in the middle of the night?" she muttered sleepily. "You got it, didn't you? Your divorce decree."

Another pause. Longer this time. She could hear him release a tautly held breath, the sound filled with pain and regret and who knew what else.

"Yeah. Yeah, I did." His voice was soft. Rough. "How did you know?"

"I saw the envelope from your lawyer when I put the mail on your desk this morning. It had the kind of portentous weight you'd expect of a divorce decree."

He chuckled, but she could hear the effort it took. Then he sighed again and she could hear the faint sound of fingers rubbing stubbled cheeks.

She could imagine him sitting there, lights off, staring into the darkness with the thin sheets of paper in his fingers. When he'd first slit the envelope and pulled the pages out, he'd have figured it was no big deal. Would have fingered through the thick wad of documents carelessly, telling himself he didn't care, that he was over Judith anyway, had been for over a year and a half now. That he could handle it. That, hell, it was the second time, after all, so he was an old hand at it. That he was too blasé, too jaded, too damned *cool* to feel anything but impatient relief that it was finally finished.

But the pain would have been there. It ran too deep, was too complicated, for it not to hurt. Even this time. And so, much later, he'd have sat there in the vast emptiness of the big house, listening to the whisper of the air-conditioning and the sound of his own heart, alone, and would have felt the quiet and the solitude and the memories close in on him. And then, finally, he'd have reached for the phone.

She squeezed her eyes closed. She was *not* going to give in this time and traipse all the way out there to hold his hand and tell him she was sorry it hadn't worked out and that everything would be all right. Not this time. Not anymore.

"How about jumping into some clothes and coming out?" he asked quietly. "We'll pour ourselves a drink and toast old times and you can help me throw the rest of her pictures out."

"It's four-thirty in the morning, Connor," Andie said through gritted teeth. She was *not* going out there, damn it. "And you sound as though you've been toasting old times half the night already. Put the cap back on that bottle of bourbon sitting on the table beside you, toss that picture of Judith you're holding into the fire and go to bed. We'll talk in the office in the morning."

"Damn!" He laughed softly, the husky, honey-warm sound wrapping around her like a silken web. "You scare me sometimes, lady. But you're only half-right—it's a bottle of twelve-year-old Scotch on the table beside me, not bourbon."

In spite of herself, Andie had to smile. "Well, I'm glad to hear you're handling things with a little class this time, Devlin. When Liza divorced you, you got drunk on cheap wine, threw up five or six times and were hung over for three days."

"Yeah, well, I guess you get better at some things if you do them often enough," he said quietly. "God knows, I can't seem to get a handle on *staying* married, but I'm getting pretty damn good at the divorce part."

"Oh, Conn..." She could feel his despair right through the phone and fought to ignore it. She had to stop running to his side every time he called, had to quit—

"Andie?" It was just a whisper, filled with pain. "Andie, damn it, I need you."

Teeth gritted, she squeezed her eyes closed, every atom of her being resisting the sweet pull of his voice. "I have to be at work in four hours."

He laughed that low, teasing laugh he knew she couldn't resist. "Come on, Andie, don't be like that. What's your boss going to do—fire you?"

"I should be so lucky," she shot back murderously.

Another laugh, gently compelling. "Lighten up a little, Andie. I'll give you the day off. How's that?"

"And who's going to finish that report you need for your meeting with Desmond Beck tomorrow afternoon?"

Conn groaned. "Cancel the meeting. Hell, cancel *tomorrow*. I'll give myself the day off, too, and we'll go do something. How about sailing? You haven't been sailing with me in over a year."

"Get serious, Devlin," Andie drawled. "Getting a chance to buy out a major competitor like Becktron comes along once in a lifetime. That company's worth millions to someone with the brains—and the guts—to haul it back from near bankruptcy and put it on its feet. Are you trying to tell me that just the *thought* of pulling off a coup like that doesn't make your little entrepreneurial heart beat faster?"

"Okay, okay, no day off for either of us." He gave a weary sigh. "So bring your stuff over here with you and you can go in to work with me." He laughed softly. "Hell, Andie, you're not going to get much more sleep anyway."

Andie lay staring at the ceiling through the darkness, telling herself for the fiftieth time that she was absolutely *not* going to drag herself out of bed and go all the way out there. Not this time.

Not ever again, in fact. She was turning over a new leaf. Was giving the old Andrea Spencer the heave-ho and introducing a new improved version, one who was impervious to sweet-talking men with gray-green eyes and fetching smiles.

"Did it ever occur to you that I might not be alone?" She glared at the ceiling. "That I just *might* have better things to do at four-thirty in the morning than help you toast your ex-wives goodbye? I'm a normal twenty-nine-year-old single woman, Connor. I *do* have a life other than Devlin Electronics."

"We promised once we'd always be there for each other. Remember?" he murmured. "Not going to break a promise to a blood brother, are you? Not going to leave your best friend in the lurch when he needs you?"

Not even thinking, she ran her finger along her left thumb, feeling the ridge of scar tissue. Twenty years later and it was still there.

Blood brothers.

Then, realizing what she was doing—what *he* was doing—she slapped her open palm down onto the bed, eyes narrowing. "Damn you," she whispered furiously. "Damn you, Connor Devlin. That's not fair! I've *always* been there for you when you've needed me. All you've ever had to do was call and—"

Gotcha.

He didn't have to say anything.

Was smart enough not to.

Andie closed her eyes and blew out a long breath, swearing softly at him. A husky, warm laugh came down the line, enfolding her like a hug, and she swallowed a sigh, wondering who she'd been trying to kid, telling herself she'd be able to resist him. She never had. Not once in twenty-two years.

"An hour," she muttered ungraciously. "And put the cap on that damned Scotch, because if you're all drunk and maudlin when I get there, I swear I'll turn around and come home."

He laughed. "When was the last time you saw me maudlin, darlin'?"

"Seven years ago, when we went through this the first time," she reminded him testily. "And put on the coffee."

"Decaf?"

"High-octane." She sat up and rubbed her eyes. "You owe me for this, Devlin. Big-time!"

"Name it and it's yours, darlin'," he said with a chuckle. "Love you, lady."

And the worst part of it was—that for those few moments it took him to say the words—he probably meant them.

It didn't take her long to get over there. She pulled on her comfortable old jeans and a sweater, shoved her makeup and hairbrush in her handbag, then grabbed something suitable for work before heading for the door, grabbing her slim leather briefcase while fumbling for her car keys.

She had to be out of her mind. Yawning and shivering slightly with the cold, Andie unlocked her little red Mercedes and slipped behind the wheel, shaking her head with disgust as she put the key in the ignition and turned it.

You'd think she'd have this under control by now. After all, she wasn't a kid anymore. It was one thing to fall in love with the cute guy next door when she was ten, quite another when she was three weeks shy of her thirtieth birthday and he *still* didn't have a clue how she felt about him.

Pathetic, that's what it was, she told herself grumpily. Just damned pathetic!

It took her all of thirty minutes to get there, the usually crowded freeway wondrously empty, the back roads leading to the big house on its five acres of rambling hills overlooking the sea deserted and pitch-black.

It always gave her an odd feeling, driving up the winding laneway with its overhanging trees, the air heavy with the scent of pine and sea salt. She'd come up here the first time nearly eleven years ago, and the memories of that night were still tender.

Conn had been a twenty-one-year-old college senior when she'd left, brilliant and popular and filled with dreams. He and his best friend, Billy Soames, had been talking of quitting college and starting their own computer company, and not long after Andie had left, they'd done it. And by eleven months later, their small two-man company had become the fastest-growing software firm on the West Coast, its two young owners successful beyond their dreams and wealthier than either had ever imagined possible.

Andie smiled humorlessly as she drove up the circular driveway. The house rose dark and solid against the night sky ahead of her, the front entrance lit up like a Christmas tree for her arrival. There had been no lights on to welcome her arrival that night eleven years ago.

It had been late that night when she'd gotten here—nearly midnight. She'd come back to Seattle from New York because she couldn't stay away any longer. She had decided, finally, that she was simply going to have to take the initiative and *make* him fall in love with her, starting out with a full-fledged seduction she'd planned down to the last detail.

She hadn't called or even written to warn him that she was coming, wanting to surprise him, wanting to see the expression on his face when he opened the door and saw her standing there, champagne bottle in one hand, suitcase in the other.

Well, she'd surprised him, all right. He'd pulled the door open and had stared blankly at her for a full second, then had frowned and asked her what the hell she was doing there at midnight. Then, recovering, he'd laughed and had wrapped her in a long, warm hug and had invited her in.

He'd barely tossed her coat over a chair and had told her to sit down when a petulent female voice had called his name from the depths of the house. And before Andie could gather her startled wits together and collect her coat and leave with some measure of dignity still intact, a tall, slender blonde had drifted into the living room, tousled and sleepy-eyed.

She'd been wearing a satin housecoat and nothing else and had gazed at Andie with patent displeasure. And then Conn, grinning like a fool, had come back into the living room, put his arm around the creature, kissed her...and, without even a hint of irony, had introduced her as Liza, his wife.

Wife.

Even now, more than a decade later, Andie felt a wave of heat brush her cheeks. Mortified and furious, she'd mumbled something in reply, collected her coat and suitcase and had bolted, blinded by tears. Conn had come after her, asking her what the hell was wrong, why she wouldn't stay at least long enough to tell him what she was doing back in Seattle and where she was staying. Then Liza had called him back to her and Andie had fled into the night, stumbling into her parents' spare bedroom at one in the morning to cry her eyes out, heart broken.

If she'd had the money, she'd have been on the next plane back to New York. But she'd had too little cash and too much pride. In the end she had defiantly stayed in Seattle, finishing college, finding a good job and a nice apartment and even a boyfriend or two. And to hell with Connor Devlin and his *wife*.

That had been eleven years and two Mrs. Devlins ago and she was still here, Andie thought as she brought the Mercedes to a stop in front of his house. Oh, on the surface everything had worked out. She had a job she loved, a beautiful apartment filled with antiques and fine art, a city full of great friends, even a man who wanted to marry her. Everything but the one thing she wanted most of all.

She still didn't have Conn Devlin.

He'd left the door unlocked for her, and as Andie stepped into the dark stillness of the big foyer, she paused instinctively for a second or two, listening. But there was no hint of unfamiliar perfume on the air, no tinkle of throaty female laughter.

Grinning at her own silliness, she walked confidently through the darkness to the corridor leading to the living room, instinctively skirting the antique table on her left and the pedestal with its Ming vase on her right. It was like a second home up here, everything as familiar and comfortable as old friends, part of her because they were part of Conn. She breathed in the air deeply, loving the male overtones of wood smoke and leather and a hint of that cologne he always wore.

The huge living room was cloaked in shadows and darkness, the only light coming from the embers still glowing in the fireplace. She could see Conn sitting in the massive armchair back in the shadows, head dropped back, eyes closed, one foot on the edge of the raised stone hearth. There was a bottle of Scotch beside his foot, open, maybe a quarter gone. A half-empty glass sat on the brass-and-hardwood table near his right hand. And there were papers scattered on the floor around him, the kind of rich, heavy velum that lawyers are so fond of using when they're telling you bad news.

She stood there for a moment or two, simply looking at him, feeling the pain emanating from him. Then she slipped off her jacket and draped it over the nearest chair and walked around behind him, reaching down to gently massage his temples.

He gave a groan of pleasure and smiled, not opening his eyes. "My angel of mercy. I didn't know if you'd come or not."

"You knew damned well I would come," she told him bluntly. "I always come."

"True." He reached up and caught her left hand in his, pulling it down and kissing her inner wrist. "I don't know what I'd do without you, darlin'. You're the only thing that makes sense in my world half the time. And by God the only thing I can count on."

"Best friends, remember?" Andie said it lightly as she walked around the chair and sat on the hearth, her fingers still meshed with his. He looked tired and slightly haggard in the dim light, and his smile was only halfhearted, obviously the best he could come up with. "You look like hell,

Devlin. Have you had anything to eat tonight with that quarter bottle of Scotch?''

Conn had to smile. Opening his eyes, he turned his head to look at her, liking, as always, what he saw. Even at five-thirty in the morning, in jeans and sweater and without a hint of makeup, she looked bandbox perfect, skin glowing, that mane of thick chestnut hair spilling around her shoulders brushed and gleaming. But that was Andie, always calm and serene and in control, never letting things get to her. Not even a jackass for a best friend.

He gave her fingers a squeeze, then dropped her hand and leaned forward to brace his elbows on his knees, scrubbing his stubbled cheeks with his hands. His eyes were gritty and his tongue resembled flannel. He felt old and tired and worn around the edges, like an old sofa that's been around too long.

"I grabbed a sandwich this afternoon, I think...." His neck was stiff and he massaged it wearily. "Or maybe that was yesterday."

"Ah, the booze-and-self-pity diet," Andie said dryly. "I have an idea! Maybe I can find some she-broke-my-heart-and-done-me-wrong music on the country station and you can sing along with it. That would be fun."

"Sure glad you came over," Conn muttered, wishing his head would stop pounding. "I love it when you get all supportive and sympathetic like this."

"Hey, I'm here, aren't I?" She gave his knee a rap with her knuckles. "How many other people do you know who'd get out of a warm bed at four-thirty in the morning to come over here and listen to you moan and groan?"

"I'm not moaning and groaning," Conn said through gritted teeth. "I'm celebrating. Every man has the right to celebrate a little when his divorce comes through. I'm a free man again. If that's not reason to celebrate, I don't know what is." Except he didn't feel like celebrating, Conn thought. He felt like crawling into a deep hole. And sleeping. Sleeping for about three months straight.

"Oh, Conn." Her voice was just a whisper, and he felt the touch of her fingertips on his cheek, his temple. Then her arms slipped gently around his neck and she knelt in front of him, holding him tightly, and Conn found himself hugging her ferociously, burying his face in her neck and breathing in the warm, female scent of her as if it were a healing nectar.

"Conn, I'm sorry it didn't work out, I really am," she whispered. "I know you'd hoped it would this time. That everything would be perfect."

Conn smiled ruefully. "I'll live, darlin'. And I feel like a damned fool, dragging you over here. When I read the papers this morning I figured, hey, I'm cool—it's over and done with, and it's what we both wanted. It's not like it was some big surprise or anything. Then..." He shrugged, then kissed the side of her throat. "Hell, I don't know. I just sort of crashed, I guess. Don't ask me why. It's not as though I loved her or anything."

"You did once," Andie said softly, pulling back gently to look at him.

"Did I?" Conn heard the bitterness in his own voice.

"Well, you must have *thought* you did. Same thing."

"I've been sitting here for hours, trying to remember just what the hell I *did* feel back then. There must have been something. I mean, a man doesn't marry a woman without feeling *something*, right?" He looked at Andie seriously. "It scares me a little sometimes. This is the second time, Andie. I can live with one divorce—when I married Liza, I was still young enough to figure all you needed was spectacular sex to keep you together."

He managed a fleeting smile, as much at Andie's expression as at the memories. "But when I married Judith, I thought it was for keeps. I figured I knew what I was doing. That what we had was something that would *last*." Another smile, slightly bitter this time. "Three years later she was gone. And I still don't know what the hell went wrong. It just...faded. I remember waking up one morn-

ing and looking at her lying beside me and wishing I'd never
even met her.''

"But the sex was spectacular."

Conn had to grin. "Oh, yeah. The sex was spectacular.
Right up to the end."

Andie's gaze held his for a fraction of a second too long;
then she looked away quickly, coloring very slightly, and
stood up. "I'll, um, make you some breakfast. I hope you
put the coffee on like I told you."

"Yeah." Conn nodded absently, watching her as she
started gathering up the papers scattered around his chair.
"Yeah, the coffee's on." Remembering, with sudden, unexpected vividness, of what it had been like with *her*.

One weekend of heaven...that's how he'd always thought
of it. Three days of a kind of closeness he'd never experi-
enced before or after. It was supposed to have been a getaway ski weekend up to Mount Baker. Just the four of
them—Andie and her boyfriend, he and Sharon Newcombe.

Then Andie and her boyfriend had split up two days before they were all supposed to leave. Conn had said there
was no reason why *she* shouldn't still go, considering there
was plenty of room in the cabin they'd rented, and Sharon
had exploded, shouting something about three being a
crowd just before she stormed out, doors slamming.

So he and Andie, both smarting from love gone wrong,
had gone by themselves, although neither of them had an-
ticipated the outcome. They'd come together like gasoline
and flame and even now, twelve years later, he could feel his
body stir slightly with just the memories of it.

It had been a weekend of magic. But then they'd gotten
back to the city and college and somehow—he never was
sure why—the magic had vanished in the hustle and bustle
of everyday life. Sharon had turned up, contrite and apologetic, and it had been Andie's turn to go storming off in a
flurry of door slamming. He'd gotten that all sorted out
about the time that college had let out, and Andie had

headed down to San Francisco to take a summer job with her brother's investment firm.

He'd planned to go down after her and talk things out. But he and his college buddy, Bill Soames, started playing around with a new idea they'd had for a prototype computer, and pretty soon the summer was gone. When Andie came back, things seemed stilted and awkward between them. And then, out of the blue, she'd decided to move to New York and they'd all but lost touch with each other for almost a year.

There was a hiss of sparks in the fireplace as a log settled, and Conn blinked, impatiently shaking himself free of the memories

Andie had tossed his divorce papers on the hearth and Conn looked at them dispassionately. Strange to think it was over that easily. Three years of great sex and a few good times, nearly a year of separation while their lawyers hammered out a deal... then a handful of papers and he was single again.

It made him laugh for some reason, although God knows it wasn't even remotely funny. Still grinning humorlessly, he stood up and stretched until his muscles popped. Andie was nowhere to be seen but he could hear her in the kitchen. Suddenly he was starved. He picked up the bottle of Scotch and capped it tightly, then grabbed the half-empty glass and followed the clatter.

She was taking plates out of the dishwasher and stacking them on the counter. Conn paused by the end of the counter to watch her, enjoying the play of faded, soft denim across the rounded contours of her trim little bottom. That was one thing he didn't see enough of these days. Hiring Andie to work with him had been smart in a lot of ways, but it also meant that she spent most of her time with him dressed in business garb.

Which was a damned shame, he found himself suddenly thinking. A real damned shame...

He set the glass on the counter, then slipped both arms around her and nuzzled the side of her throat. "You know what I was just thinking?" he purred against her ear.

"I'm afraid to ask."

"I was just thinking that we *could* take the day off. The Becktron deal can wait a day or two—if anything, it'll just make Desmond Beck more agreeable." Her skin was slightly salty, and Conn ran the tip of his tongue around the lobe of her ear, feeling her give a tiny start. He wondered why he'd never done this before. Hell, it wasn't as though the idea hadn't occurred to him now and again. But it just never seemed…well, right, somehow, making a pass at your best friend.

"Connor…" There was a hint of alarm in her voice.

"I have another idea, too," he murmured, running one hand gently up under her sweater and settling his palm on warm, bare flesh, caressing her gently.

"Conn…" She'd stiffened at the first touch of his hand on her abdomen, as though not entirely believing what he was doing.

"We could go to bed for an hour or two," he whispered, slipping the fingers of his left hand under the waistband of her jeans while letting his right glide up to lightly touch her breasts through silk and lace. They were warm and full and he remembered how sensitive they'd been those long twelve years ago, how she'd groaned softly when he'd—

"Connor…!" Breathless with surprise, she recoiled back against him.

"God, you feel good," he growled, filling his hands with the incredible softness and warmth of her. "I'd forgotten how good you feel, Andie." Nuzzling her throat, he splayed his fingers across her belly and pulled her against him, pressing gently against her, already fully aroused.

"Remember what it was like that weekend up at Mount Baker?" He felt her breath catch very slightly and smiled, running his fingertips along the edge of her bra and hoping she still wore the kind that fastened in front, smiling again

when he discovered that she did. "We could have that kind
of magic again, Andie. We could—"

"Conn, wh-what are you *doing?*" Her voice was just a
dazed whisper.

"What the hell do you think I'm doing?" he asked with
a throaty chuckle. "It's been a while, but I think it's called
foreplay...."

He thought about what it had been like, making love to
Andie that first time, wild and vital and so hungry for each
other they'd practically gone up in smoke.

Twelve years later, and he could remember that first long
silken slide into heaven as though it had happened no more
than an hour ago. Could still hear the soft noise she'd made
deep in her throat, the way her body had taken him, wel-
comed him, loved him as he'd pressed deep, deep...slaking
himself in the hot, satin depths of her.

Conn groaned and moved against her. The catch on her
bra gave way easily. He caressed her breasts, the nipples
hard against his palm, and he could hear her moan very
softly as he rubbed them, teased them.

She'd grabbed his wrist and he felt her fingers tighten
convulsively. He remembered what it had been like with her
twelve years ago, how she'd gasped with pleasure the first
time he'd taken one taut nipple into his mouth, sucking it,
caressing it with his tongue.

He remembered other things, too...touching her for the
very first time, fingers seeking, finding, teasing. The way
she'd pressed her thighs together, embarrassed and a little
uncertain, until finally, with a soft sigh of raw pleasure,
she'd relaxed and had let him ease his hand under the narrow bikini panties she'd been wearing. She'd been fire and
honey and hot silken need, and in no time at all she'd arched
against his hand, eyes wide with shock and delight.

The knot in his belly tightened, and he moved against her
again, pressing himself against her round, denim-clad bottom and feeling his own breath catch. He slipped the metal
button on her waistband free and tugged the zipper down

impatiently, slipping his hand inside to cup the feminine curve of her belly before sliding down and beneath the band of her panties. "Andie, I want you...." he groaned, moving evocatively against her.

"Connor!" The word was little more than a gasp. "P-please!"

Growling something, he drew his hand from her and turned her in his arms, pressing her back against the dishwasher, one thigh pressing between hers even as he slipped his fingers into her hair. Tipping her face up, he brought his mouth down over hers, tongue sliding deep, seeking hers, finding it, as familiar and welcoming as coming home. She kissed him back, her arms going around his neck, lithe body arching against his....

And then, very suddenly, she wrenched her mouth away and turned her face so he couldn't kiss her again, planting both hands on his shoulders and pushing him firmly away. "Damn it, Connor, what the *hell* do you think you're doing?"

"Kissing you," he muttered, trying to do it again. "Damn it, Andie, quit turning away and—"

"*Stop* it!"

She was stronger than he would have guessed and she shoved him back roughly, panting for breath, cheeks flushed, eyes snapping. Giving her head a toss to get her tousled hair out of her eyes, she glared up at him. "Back off!"

"Andie, for the love of—!" Swearing, he took a step back, blood hammering in his temples, so aroused it hurt just to stand there, breathing hard. "What's wrong? What the hell is—?"

"I am *not* some vacant pair of hips you can just use when the mood strikes you, mister! If you need to reaffirm your manhood or drown your sorrows or celebrate your newfound bachelor status or whatever the hell it is you're doing, fine—but *not* with *me!*"

"What?" Conn just stared down at her, mind spinning with confusion. "Honey, that's not what—"

"No!" Mouth tight with fury, she glowered right back up at him, wrenching the gaping fly of her jeans closed, then reaching under her sweater and fastening her bra. "Is that why you called me over here tonight? Because you're feeling a little sorry for yourself and figure all you need to get over the divorce blues is a good—"

"Don't even say it," he growled, raking his fingers through his hair. "Look, I—" Swearing ferociously, he wheeled away and planted his hands on the edge of the counter, letting his head sag, eyes closed. "I'm sorry," he muttered finally. "Damn it, Andie, I'm sorry. I don't know what..." He shook his head.

And he didn't know, he realized glumly. Sure, now and again he'd thought about what it would be like to make love to her again, but it was more out of idle curiosity than any real sense of desire. She was *Andie,* for crying out loud. His best friend. And a person didn't hit on his best friend!

"I'm sorry, too," she said finally, sounding subdued. "It was... Let's just forget it, okay? It's five-thirty in the morning, I'm tired, you're a little drunk...."

Her small hand settled warmly between his shoulder blades, moving in soothing circles. "You're my best friend, Devlin. That doesn't mean I won't punch your lights out if you try something like this again, but let's not make a big deal out of it, okay?" She leaned close and kissed him lightly on the cheek, her breast pressing against his arm for a fleeting moment. "Go take a shower—a *cold* shower. I'll make some breakfast."

In spite of himself, Conn had to grin. Straightening, he reached out and caught her by the hand as she started to step away. "Why don't you come with me? Hell, darlin', it's been twelve years since we shared a shower. There are worse ways to start a morning."

"You're pushing your luck, Devlin," she replied mildly, planting her outstretched fingers in the middle of his chest and holding him firmly at bay.

He smiled down at her, wondering what he'd ever done to deserve a woman like this in his life. Even at arm's length, she was the best thing that had ever happened to him. "If I'd had any damn sense at all, I'd have married you eleven years ago instead of Liza," he said half-seriously.

She hesitated for just a split second, an odd expression crossing her face. Then she smiled carelessly. "And ruin a perfectly good friendship, Devlin? We nearly did that by sleeping together that weekend up at Mount Baker. Remember?"

"Oh, I remember," he said with a growl.

"And if you remember all of it, we agreed that our friendship was more important than sex. And that—"

"Spectacular sex," he amended straight-faced. "We *did* agree it was pretty spectacular sex, Andie."

"Yes, all right, *spectacular* sex." She was trying not to laugh. "But we agreed that good friends are harder to find than lovers, remember. Even *good* lovers."

"*Great* lovers, even," he agreed blandly.

"Great?" She looked pleasantly surprised. "You really thought I was—?" She caught herself abruptly. Shrugging offhandedly, she stepped past him, avoiding his eyes. "Go take a shower, Devlin."

"Yes, ma'am." Grinning, he headed for the kitchen door. "And yeah, you *were* great. Once we got past all the virginal inhibitions, darlin', you were—"

"Censor that," she said quickly, suddenly very busy rummaging through the refrigerator. "Eggs...bread... How about French toast for breakfast?"

"I'm easy."

"I've noticed."

"Feel free to take advantage of it."

"You wish."

Sometimes, Conn found himself thinking, glancing at her with an unexpected twinge of wistfulness. *Sometimes I do wish, darlin'....*

But he couldn't say it aloud, of course. Not to his best friend.

Two
_____

Staying there—setting the glass-topped rattan table in the big sun room off the kitchen, making French toast, pouring orange juice—was one of the hardest things Andie had ever done.

Every instinct she had was telling her to run. To hide. To shut herself up in her apartment and pull the covers over her head and simply die of mortification.

One touch—that's all it had taken. One touch and she'd all but melted in his arms like overheated taffy, as pliant and eager as any teenager. Where she'd found the strength to push him away, she'd never know. Because she hadn't wanted to. All she'd wanted was for him to strip her out of her jeans and ease her down onto the floor and make love to her as though his very life depended on it.

Shoving a handful of tangled hair off her forehead, she took a deep breath and wet her lips, closing her eyes for a calming minute. It was all right. She could handle this.

The secret was to stay cool and simply pretend it had meant nothing. Nothing at all.

Conn wasn't drunk, but he'd had more to drink than normal. He'd been hurting, vulnerable, off balance—all alien emotions for a man who prided himself on his pragmatic and levelheaded approach to life. She'd been there, warm and female and reassuringly familiar. His best friend, his confidant, the one person who probably knew him better than anyone. What more normal thing to do than reach for her, seeking to put his world right again through the comforting rituals of lovemaking?

Odds were that he wouldn't even remember the incident in a day or two.

So no harm had been done.

As long as *she* kept the whole incident in perspective, she reminded herself grimly. As long as she didn't try to delude herself into believing that Conn, with blinding insight that had eluded him for twelve years, had suddenly recognized that she was the only woman for him.

Feeling more in control, she added a few drops of vanilla and a sprinkle of sugar to the cream and eggs, then started beating them with a wire whisk. It was time, she told herself calmly. In three weeks, she was going to be thirty years old. Too old to still believe in miracles. It was time she shook herself free of Conn once and for all and got on with her life, because she would be *damned* if she was going to turn into one of those silly calf-eyed women who waits and waits and waits…and then one day wakes up to realize that an entire lifetime has slipped by and her dreams have turned to dust.

The French toast had cooked to a deep golden brown by the time Andie heard the shower go off. A couple of minutes later Conn padded into the kitchen in a waft of soap-scented steam, cleanly shaven and barefoot, dressed in a ragged old pair of denim cutoffs and nothing else. He was still fit and lean, she noticed idly, his shoulders still solid, belly still flat and hard. And he could still make her heart give that silly little leap with just one lazy grin.

Ignoring it, she simply smiled. "You look almost human again. Feel better?"

"Actually, I feel like a damned fool," he muttered. Walking across to her, he bent down to give her a chaste—and chastened—peck on the cheek. "Sorry. I don't know what the hell I thought I was doing, grabbing you like that. I didn't mean anything by it."

As she knew all too well, Andie thought wearily. "Forget it, Devlin," she told him easily. "You're a man. Men do stupid things all the time. It's what makes you so endearing." Refusing to think about it, she slid three thick slices of French toast onto a warmed plate and handed it to him. "Eat this. You still look a little rough around the edges."

"Feel a little rough around the edges." Grinning, he took the plate and padded into the sun room, raking his fingers through his wet hair. "I still can't believe I had the brass to haul you out of bed and all the way out here just because I was feeling sorry for myself."

"You're allowed," she replied casually, carrying her own plate across to the table and sitting down. "Most of the time you're an intelligent, competent businessman with a solid grasp on his life and destiny. I figure you're entitled to one night of generalized stupidity, all considered. Just don't make a habit of it."

Conn winced slightly. "Point taken. Still friends?"

"Forever." She said it easily, the ritual as old as their friendship.

Conn just nodded, prodding the French toast thoughtfully. He'd been thinking about Andie in the shower—a few salacious thoughts, granted, but it had been more than that. Thinking about how she was always there for him, about how he sometimes just took for granted that all he had to do was shout and she'd be there, calm and collected and in control.

"You, uh..." He looked at her thoughtfully. "You didn't *really* have someone with you when I called tonight, did you?"

Andie stared at him, fork halfway to her mouth. "What a question to ask!"

"You would tell me, wouldn't you? If you were getting serious about someone?"

"It's the strangest thing...." Andie cocked her head slightly, as though listening to something. "I could swear I hear my mother. Didn't that just sound like my mother?"

"All right, all right," he growled. "I know it's none of my business, but—"

"It *is* my mother!" She looked around with exaggerated surprise. "I was *sure* she was in Portland this week."

"Don't be a wise guy," Conn muttered. "I'm dead serious, Andie." Realizing, with some surprise, that he meant it. "We've never kept secrets from each other. I know you and that French banker, André or Albert or whatever his name is, have been seeing a lot of each other lately."

She leaned back with an exaggerated sigh, crossing her arms. "I presume you mean Alain DeRocher, the French-Canadian investment analyst *you* introduced me to last year. Yes, we have been seeing each other pretty often, or as often as possible, considering I live on one side of the continent and he lives on the other. And no, he wasn't with me tonight. Nor was anyone else, for that matter. Happy?"

Conn gave a grunt, only half-mollified. "So you and he aren't . . . ?" He lifted his eyebrow eloquently.

"Connor!" She gave a burst of laughter. "It's none of your business if we are!" Still grinning, she looked at him with amusement. "Although, to forestall any more questioning, no, we are not—yet," she added slyly.

"Yet." Conn's eyes narrowed slightly. "Meaning he's thinking about it."

"Of course he's thinking about it—he's French!"

"And you'd . . . ?" He lifted his eyebrow again.

"Now that's *really* none of your business!"

"So you're thinking about it, too."

"Connor!" Andie took a deep breath, then let it out again with a quiet laugh. "I bet he would at least bring me flowers and wine before trying to peel me out of my jeans."

Conn winced. "I said I was sorry about that, damn it."

"Mmm." She looked at him for a moment, an odd expression on her face. "What I'm saying, Conn, is that I just don't know how I feel about him. He's certainly everything a woman could want...."

Conn gave a grunt, not liking the expression on her face. Not liking the idea of DeRocher trying to peel her out of a damned thing, flowers or no flowers. "He's too old for you."

Andie's left eyebrow arched indolently. "Excuse me?"

"Well, hell, he's got to be fifty if he's a day."

"Forty-one."

"Like I said, he's too old for you."

"I like older men." There was a dangerous glow in her eyes.

"He's probably married."

"He's never been married."

"Never?" It was Conn's turn to lift his eyebrow. "Don't you think that's damn strange? That this perfect specimen of a man has never been married? Doesn't that tell you something?"

"It tells me," she said sweetly, "that he is considerably wiser that some men I could mention."

"Sounds to me as though he's got some sort of problem. In the fun-and-games department, I mean."

"Trust me," Andie shot back even more sweetly. "He has no problem in that area at all."

"I don't even want to know how you've figured that out if you haven't even—"

"Didn't you tell me just last week that you don't have to take a boat out to know whether it's going to handle well in heavy weather or not? Gut instinct, I think you said."

"I also mentioned experience," Conn said silkily. "And I think I've had a bit more experience with sailboats than you've had with—"

"Do you have *any* idea at all of how thin that ice is where you're standing?"

Conn grinned, cutting into the French toast with his fork. "Hey, I was just trying to make a point. If you like the guy, fine . . . go with what feels good. Just don't start getting serious about him or anything, though, because—"

"He's asked me to marry him."

She said it quietly, without laughter or even a sly smile to soften it, and Conn nearly choked on a mouthful of toast. "He's *what?*" His bellow made her blink. "Marry you? He can't marry you! It's out of the damned question!"

"And just why is it out of the question?"

"Because . . ." He didn't know for certain, Conn realized, but there was no *damned* way he was going to let Andie, *his* Andie, marry some no-good French-Canadian financier and— "Your job, for one thing," he said with satisfaction. "He lives in Montreal. Your job is here. The commute is a killer."

"Alain lives in Quebec City," she said calmly. "His ancestral home is there—all forty-seven rooms of it. His head office is in Montreal, but he's only there a couple of days a week."

"Even worse," Conn growled. "Quebec City is even farther away."

"I'd quit my job, obviously."

"Over my dead body."

"Easily enough arranged, Mr. Devlin."

"You're my best friend. You can't move to Canada—what would I do without you?"

Something flickered across her face, gone before he could figure out what it was. "You'll manage, Conn. You always do."

"That's not the point." He felt unsettled and angry for no real reason, and he frowned at her, reaching out suddenly to run his finger down the silken sweep of her hair. "You're not *really* going to marry him, are you, Andie?"

"I don't know what you'd have to say about it if I did." She sounded impatient and a little angry herself, and there was a hint of color across her cheekbones. "I have a life of my own, Connor. You seem to forget that sometimes. I have a right to be happy. My entire existence doesn't revolve around you, you know."

Conn looked across the table at her, trying to read her expression. "Are you saying you're not happy?" He mulled the thought over, trying to make some sense of it. "Are you saying—?"

"I'm not saying anything," she snapped, stabbing a piece of French toast with her fork. "It's just that sometimes I think you don't see me as a person at all. I'm just good old Andie, best friend and blood brother. I take care of your office, make your dental appointments, hire and fire your cleaning staff, pick up your dry cleaning. I make sure you get to meetings on time, that your jet's fueled up and ready to go when you need it, that your library books get back on time."

She put the fork down with a bang and looked up at him angrily. "My God, I don't know why you even *bother* getting married. I do everything a wife does, without any of the hassles of divorce!"

Conn simply stared at her, trying to figure out just what the hell he should be saying. Knowing that whatever it was, it had better be good. He hadn't seen her like this in a long time, had no idea what had set her off. "Look, Andie," he said carefully, feeling his way gingerly through a verbal mine field, "I know I can be—"

"Forget it." She shoved her chair back and stood up, cheeks flushed slightly. "I know what you're going to say, and you're right. You *can* be a selfish, arrogant bastard at times. But this isn't about you, it's about me. I—"

She stopped abruptly, then just shrugged and managed a rough smile. "Oh, don't look so alarmed, Conn—I'm not

going to run off to Canada and marry Alain DeRocher or
quit my job or throw dishes or anything. I'm just tired and
I needed to let off some steam. Finish your breakfast while
I take a shower, and I promise that by the time I come out
I'll be back to normal."

"Hey, Andie?" Conn got to his feet in one easy move,
reaching out to grab her arm gently as she turned to leave.
"Hey, darlin', I'm sorry. I had no right dragging you out of
bed to come over here and hold my hand. And I sure as hell
have no right trying to tell you who you should or shouldn't
date or marry or sleep with or whatever. If you want to do
the nasty with old DeRocher, hey—you've got my bless-
ing."

For a split second, Andie was seriously tempted to plant
her open palm across his cheek with every bit of strength she
possessed just to see if *that* would shake him up a bit. But
even as the urge hit her, it vanished again, leaving her
struggling not to laugh with the sheer impossibility of the
man. "No wonder women fall all over themselves to marry
you, Connor Devlin," she finally said. "You're the most
romantic devil I've met in years!"

Still laughing, she turned and left him standing there with
a perplexed expression on his handsome face, suddenly
afraid that if she stayed in the room with him for even another instant, she'd burst into tears.

Four hours, three cups of coffee and a crisis or two later,
Andie was still having trouble concentrating, the memory of
Conn's strong, muscled body pressed intimately against hers
just a little too vivid for comfort.

She'd be fine for a while, her mind focused on work with
its usual laserlike intensity, but then she'd remember the
warmth of his breath on her throat or the way his rough-
ened palm had cradled her breast. Without warning, her
breath would catch and her thoughts would go leaping off
into all sorts of inappropriate directions, and she'd find
herself sitting at her desk, staring blankly at some piece of

paper, or look up and see someone looking down at her expectantly and realize they'd asked her a question she hadn't even heard.

"If I didn't know better," her secretary finally said with an all-too-shrewd look, "I'd say you'd spent the night in the sack with some seriously bodacious guy, drinking champagne and making love until the sun came up."

"Champagne gives me the hiccups," Andie replied with a laugh, tossing down a handful of papers, "and I never make love until sunup the night before I have to put the finishing touches on a buy-out offer worth millions." She grinned. "Seriously bodacious, huh? From that, am I given to understand that your daughter is home from college for spring break?"

Margie Bakerfield grinned back. "Like, for real, dude. It's been three days now, and I haven't understood a word she's said. It's frightening when you think about it. I'm spending several thousand dollars to send a perfectly normal, well-spoken girl to the best college in California. And she comes back speaking in tongues, with no visible tan line and a boyfriend whose main interests seem to be food and surfing."

"Oh, to be young and in love, Margie. Let her enjoy it. When I was eighteen I thought the world would stay a magic place forever. Now I'm almost thirty, and the only magic I seem able to conjure up is time-shifting old movies on my VCR."

"That Frenchman of yours looks like he should be able to conjure up a thing or two," Margie said slyly. "He called this morning and wants you to call him back. The number's here on your desk somewhere."

Andie nodded absently, leafing through a thick computer printout. "Has Finance sent down their revised estimates on this Becktron deal yet? Conn and I are going head-to-head with Desmond Beck and his head bean counter on Friday. We need to have a solid handle on how much their patents are worth before Conn goes in with his final offer."

Margie reached across Andie's desk without saying anything and tapped in a couple of commands on the computer. It flashed a Working message for a moment or two, then spilled a multicolored display of figures across the screen.

Andie gazed at it in silence, then glanced up at Margie with a rueful smile. "I knew that."

Margie just nodded, a tiny smile playing around her mouth. "Come over to supper some night this week, okay? You and Krista can swap stories about college life—she thinks I'm too old to remember back that far."

Andie gave a sputter of laughter. Margie was all of thirty-eight. "Sounds good—pick an evening and tell me when."

"Thursday. Right after work."

"I thought you were going to the symphony on Thursday night with that new guy in Product Design."

"Brad?" Margie made a face. "We went out twice. The first time, he took me to a romantic restaurant and spent the entire evening telling me all about his ex-wives. The second time, we went to a computer show and he spent the entire *day* telling me all about his mother. The third time he called, I told him I was washing the dog. He hasn't called again."

Andie groaned, laughing. "Oh, Margie, I'm sorry! I sometimes think all the unattached men in this city come in two flavors—weird and seriously weird."

Margie smiled dryly. "You got that right." The smile faded. "And the ones who aren't just don't seem to be able to see what's right in front of them."

She could have been talking about Conn, Andie thought, but she wasn't. Only Frank Czarnecki could put that look of gloom on Margie's usually cheerful face. "You could ask him over to dinner," she said gently. "Or to a movie."

"I know," Margie said with a sigh. "If only he wasn't so shy! I think he's interested, Andie, I really do. But he doesn't seem to know what to do about it. Until I met Frank, I didn't know what a computer nerd *was!* It's all he seems to care about."

"Back when Conn and I were in college, most of his friends were just like Frank," Andie said sympathetically. "If a girl even looked at them, they'd stammer and drop things. Most of them started their own computer companies and are bazillionaires by now, but they still have the social skills of fungi. It goes with the territory."

"Except for Connor."

"Except for Connor." Andie smiled. "He always did have more going for him than a triple-digit IQ. He went from grade school charmer directly to corporate tycoon and bypassed the nerd stage altogether."

Margie paused, as though wanting to add something. Then she just smiled. "Thursday evening, then. Mexican?"

"Love it."

"Good. I'll stock up on salsa and chili peppers and make it a night to remember. Krista's boyfriend, Tad, will be there, but he's an easy conversationalist. One grunt means no, two means yes and a shrug means he doesn't know."

"He doesn't talk?"

"Who knows? I've never seen him with his mouth empty long enough to find out."

"I can hardly wait to meet him. He sounds like some of the guys I used to date when I was Krista's age." Laughing, Andie pushed back her chair and got to her feet, grabbing up a handful of reports from the corner of her desk. "I have to go over these with Conn. Hold my calls—unless it's someone from Becktron."

"Did, um . . . ?" Margie winced. "I saw that official-looking envelope from his lawyer in yesterday's mail. . . ."

"His divorce decree. Signed, sealed and as final as they get."

"So, he's single again. I suppose that means that Woodruff female will have her claws in him." Margie's eyes glittered. "For months now, she's been hovering around like a vulture waiting for an accident to happen. You can practically hear her salivating at the prospect of hauling in the catch of the day."

Margie's metaphors may have been mixed, but they made their point. "If she's serious about landing him, she's going to have to bring in the heavy-duty tackle," Andie said quietly. "One sign she's getting serious and he'll head for open water."

"Let's hope you're right." Picking up a handful of letters she'd brought in for Andie to sign, Margie turned and headed back to her own office.

Andie stared blindly after her for a moment or two, then gave herself a mental shake and walked across to the door leading to Conn's office. Olivia Woodruff. Interesting thought.

Shrewd, beautiful and as cold as ice, she headed up one of the most successful corporate law offices on the West Coast. She'd wooed Conn for almost a year before he'd shifted Devlin Electronics over to her, and she'd never bothered hiding the fact that Conn's business wasn't all she was interested in. So far, Conn had held her at bay. But now...?

Andie was still frowning when she gave a tap on Conn's door, then pushed it open and went in.

Conn's office ran the full width of the building, a peaceful retreat filled with antiques and fine art, with plenty of polished dark wood and gleaming brass and leather. Her doing, of course. Had it been left up to Conn, he'd still have nothing in here but a dozen custom-wired computers, a phone and a stack of discarded pizza boxes.

She smiled. Under the expensive suits and hundred-dollar haircuts still lurked that frighteningly bright college kid whose passion for electronics had given birth to a thriving corporation worth millions.

"Hey, darlin'," he croaked, looking up as she came in.

"You look in fine shape," Andie replied calmly. "Head hurts, does it?"

Conn managed a groan, then wished he hadn't. He closed his eyes—gently—and gingerly rubbed both temples. "I didn't think twelve-year-old Scotch gave you a hangover."

She disappeared behind him and poured something into a glass. "Consumed in reasonable quantities, I don't think it does."

"Cheap shot."

"Easy, anyway." She set something on the desk. "Drink up."

Conn opened one eye and gazed blearily at the glass of bubbling liquid in front of him. "Quick or slow?"

"Quick. It tastes like hell."

"Is it going to kill me or cure me?"

"Do you really care?"

"No." Sitting back in his leather chair with another groan, Conn reached for the glass and downed the contents in three long swallows, giving a shudder as it hit bottom. "You're enjoying this, aren't you?"

"Just a little." Smiling, she strolled around behind him and settled her hands on his shoulders, kneading them gently. "Take a couple of deep breaths and repeat after me. I will never drink Scotch on an empty stomach again."

"Don't mention Scotch," Conn groaned. "Don't mention stomach."

"I set up a meeting with Production at eleven. I called Frank Czarnecki and asked him to bring his whole design team with him."

Conn started to nod, then thought better of it, relaxing against the warmth of her hands and feeling her fingers work through the knots across his shoulders. "So we're still having quality-control problems with that remote-controlled underwater seismic unit. Damn!"

"They're running at a fifty percent reject rate, with no sign it's improving. Frank swears the problem isn't with the design, but with something in the manufacturing process."

"And Production swears the problem's in the design." Conn flexed his shoulders, wincing slightly as a jolt of pain shot through his skull. "That design is sound, Andie. I went over the schematics with Frank six dozen times. The damn thing *should* work. The prototype met every test way above specification."

"So there's a bug in the manufacturing process," Andie said thoughtfully.

"Seems so. Wherever the hell it is, though, we've got to track it down fast. DeepSix Exploration has just signed a billion-dollar oil exploration contract with the Canadian government and needs those remote units *now*. We can't sell them a product that might work half the time, and they're not going to wait around while we try to figure out what's going wrong."

He groaned again, this time in frustration, and tipped his head forward so she could massage the nape of his neck. "What's your take on the situation?"

"Our design and production teams are the best in the business, but they mistrust each other on principle. What if they're spending so much time blaming each *other* for the problem that they're overlooking something else? Something no one's thought of yet."

"Such as?"

"I don't know." The rhythmic motion of her fingers paused as she thought about it, then resumed their slow massage of his neck muscles. "Some element in the manufacturing process that neither has control over. Something *we* don't make. Something that comes in from the outside that—"

"The system program chip." Forgetting his aching head, Conn sat straight up. "We subcontract it from Schoendorf Systems for less than it would cost to make it ourselves."

"So what if there's some sort of sporadic manufacturing problem at Shoendorf's end? It's possible that flawed chips are getting through our spot checks and into our units. That would explain why only some are faulty, while others are fine."

Conn was already reaching for the phone. "I'm going down to the production floor to talk with Bob Miller. You call the warehouse and have them send over a random sampling of chips—pronto. We'll test the little suckers this afternoon."

"On it," Andie said, already heading for the door. "I'll call Shoendorf and have them fax over copies of all their quality-control tests for the last six months. I'll also see if they've changed suppliers. Maybe the problem is farther up the line."

Grinning, Conn watched Andie as she strode across the room and out the door, his hangover miraculously gone. "Tell that Frenchman of yours if he wants to marry you, he'll have to go through me to do it," he called after her. *You're mine!*

Hell, he'd be bankrupt without her, he thought idly as he waited for someone down in Production to pick up the phone. It chilled him a little, just the thought of losing her.

There was no one else in the company whose judgment he trusted as much as he trusted hers. She didn't just know the business inside out; she knew him just as intimately, able to finish his thoughts for him while he was still struggling to put an idea into words, able to follow his leaps of logic when he was sorting through a problem while everyone else stood around trying to figure out what he was talking about.

She was his sounding board when he needed to talk an idea through, and had enough solid ideas of her own that he'd learned to listen when she had something to say. She could cut through the clutter to the heart of a problem faster than anyone he knew, too, playing devil's advocate when she needed to, knowing which questions to ask, which issues to raise.

Besides, unlike most of the people who worked for him, she wasn't afraid of him. She tolerated his occasional lapses in temper, ignored his bellows of impatience, told him to shut up now and again when she got tired of listening to him rant and rave over some problem.

He had to grin. Everyone else just ran for cover and lay low until the storm blew over. But Andie always seemed to take things—and him—in stride, rarely rattled, never confused, a small spot of calm in an otherwise chaotic world.

He thought of holding her this morning. Of how she'd felt in his arms, all female softness and warmth, of the taste of her skin, her hair, her mouth. It had surprised him a little, how right she'd felt there. And his strong response had surprised him just as badly; he hadn't realized until then just how damned sexy she was, how much he'd enjoy making love to her again.

How much he'd enjoyed it twelve years ago, he reminded himself with an inward smile. Strange, how a man could forget something like that until it all came rushing back, every detail of it, of her, so clear it could have been merely a night ago.

He realized what he was doing suddenly and sat upright with a breathed oath, irritated at his own wandering thoughts. He had to stop this. She'd kill him if she even *suspected* he was thinking of that night more than a decade ago, let alone remembering it in fond detail.

And this morning. This morning had nearly been the mistake of his life.

It had been too easy, reaching for her like that. Too comfortable. Granted, it had been a hell of a long dry spell since Judith had walked out, but a little sexual deprivation hadn't killed a man yet. Simple lust was no excuse to ruin the best friendship he'd ever had or *would* ever have, so unless he was prepared to lose Andie completely, he had to make damned sure he kept things strictly business between them from now on.

Andie glanced at her watch, frowning at how quickly the morning was slipping by. Bob Miller and Frank Czarnecki would be in the third-floor meeting room in another half hour. And if she wasn't there to referee, they'd be at each other's throats in minutes, each convinced the other was responsible for the seismic unit's dismal failure rate on the assembly line.

It wasn't that neither wanted to take responsibility, it was just that both felt more loyalty to Devlin Electronics—and Conn—than they did to each other. They wanted the DeepSix seismic project to work. And took it very personally when it didn't.

Her phone gave a subdued chime and she reached for it absently, doing some quick mental calculations on the new production figures for that gigantic order of memory boards they were putting together for a well-known computer company. On schedule and under budget, so far. She made a mental note to congratulate Bob Miller.

"Andie," Margie said into her ear, "trouble's on its way."

"Trouble?" Instinctively, Andie looked up at her office door. "Who and what?"

"Killer shark," Margie said with a chuckle. "Good luck."

"Killer *what?*" But Margie had put the receiver down with a click, and before Andie could figure out what on earth she was talking about, her office door swung open and a swirl of red silk, swinging blond hair and expensive perfume came through.

Andie felt her hackles rise. "Good morning, Olivia. It's nice to see you."

"I doubt that," Olivia Woodruff said with a quiet laugh. She smiled down at Andie. "Protective little enclave you have here, isn't it? I have to practically submit to a strip search to get a visitor's badge from Security, then I have to fight my way by Margie to get in here, then by you to see Connor."

Smiling with equal warmth—that is to say, none at all—Andie leaned well back in her chair, legs crossed, and eyed the intruder calmly. "I'd tell you to go right in, but he's not here."

"In a meeting, I suppose." Olivia's eyes drifted toward the door to Conn's office, as though suspecting a lie.

"No, he's down on the production floor somewhere."

"And I suppose having him paged is out of the question?"

"I wouldn't suggest it. He doesn't like being interrupted when he's busy."

"Not even for me?" The smile was bold. The eyes above it bolder.

"Not even for me." Check and mate.

"Mmm. Serious indeed." Olivia's smile was as cool as her pale blue eyes.

As always, she was dressed for battle, clad in purple silk trousers and a coordinating purple-and-apple-green blouse, over which she'd carelessly tossed a brilliant red silk jacket. The effect was dazzling and expensive and probably created whiplash up and down the street as she passed by.

"So, our mutual friend is single again, I hear."

"I don't discuss Mr. Devlin's personal business, Olivia," Andie said with a smile. "You should know that by now."

"True. Getting information out of you is like prying money out of one of my ex-husbands." Shoving her hands in her jacket pockets, she gazed down at Andie companionably. "I suppose it's only courtesy to advise you that I have designs on him."

Andie bit back a hostile reply and smiled gently. "Well, then I suppose it's only fair to tell you that you're just one of many, Olivia." She was amused to see a flicker of annoyance deep in the other woman's eyes. She let her smile widen. "I figure by the time word gets around, he'll be knee-deep in women with designs comparable to yours."

Olivia didn't smile back. "And what about you, Andrea? I get the impression you may have a design or two yourself."

"Dating the man you work for isn't good business, Olivia."

"Oh, I don't know. It's been a long while since I worked for anyone but myself, but I seem to remember that dating the boss added a bit of excitement to the day. Although I suggest that if you decide to indulge in some midday desktop lovemaking, lock the office door unless you want to startle the secretarial staff.''

Andie had to laugh. "Have you taken a good look at the top of Conn's desk lately? Making love on it would be like making love in a mine field—if you came down on one of those prototype circuit boards the wrong way, you could hurt yourself.''

To her surprise, Olivia gave a snort of genuine laughter. "God, he's like a kid with all that electronic junk, isn't he? We were in his car last week, stopped at a red light, and the next thing I know he's got his window down and is talking with a ten-year-old in the car beside him about video games!''

"If you're serious about having designs on him, you'd better get used to it. And it would be a good idea if you learned how to play some of those video games, too.''

Olivia shuddered delicately. "I don't think so, thanks.'' She displayed long-tapered fingernails painted the exact shade of red as her jacket. "I'm certain I can interest Conn in games of a more personal nature.''

Andie thought fleetingly of being in Conn's arms that morning, could still almost feel the coiled strength in his lean body as he'd pressed against her, wanting, needing....

"I have no doubt of that,'' she said with forced calm, fighting the temptation to launch herself at Olivia's slender throat. Killing Olivia wouldn't do much good in the long run. Another woman would simply take her place. Trying to keep women away from Conn was like trying to keep bees away from a picnic.

"Well...'' Olivia made an exaggerated show of looking at her watch. "I can't spend all morning here. Are you sure you can't call Conn and tell him I'm here?''

"I have no idea where he is,'' Andie said quite truthfully. "It could take twenty minutes to track him down, and even then there's no guarantee he'll stop whatever he's doing to take my call. You said it yourself—he's like a kid when it comes to electronic gadgets. And the production floor is like a gigantic toy shop. He could be down there all afternoon.''

Olivia's expression darkened and she glared at the door to his office impotently. ''Tell him I was here, will you?''

''Of course. Does he have your number?'' Low shot.

It earned her a cool look. ''You know he does, Andrea. And trust me, honey—I have yours.'' Countershot.

Andie had her mouth open to make a pointed retort when the door banged open and Conn strode in, grinning broadly. He had his expensively tailored suit jacket tossed carelessly over one broad shoulder, the top two buttons of his Armani shirt undone, hundred-dollar tie hanging loose around his neck. There was a smudge of grease on his shirtfront, his hair was tousled as though he'd run his fingers through it in exasperation and he was brandishing a circuit board like the Grail itself.

''You were right, darlin'! Have I told you lately that I love you?''

Three

Olivia Woodruff was leaning against the corner of Andie's desk, looking like a million dollars, as usual. She turned toward him with an expectant smile as Conn strode across the room. He gave her a nod of acknowledgment as he stepped by her and leaned down to plant a long and thoroughly satisfying kiss squarely on Andie's upturned mouth.

Trying to ignore a distinctive and erotic stirring low in his belly, he grinned and squatted beside her chair, feeling like a five-year-old on Christmas morning as he brandished the circuit board. "You got it in one, hotshot. I owe you big for this one—you probably saved us about twelve million bucks in contracts."

She grinned back, eyes sparkling. "So...it was the board."

"Nearly three months ago, Shoendorf changed suppliers for one of the components used on the board. They'd been having trouble with quality control, but no one told us about it.'' He dared to lean across to give her another swift kiss. "You've earned yourself a raise, kid.''

Andie laughed, looking as genuinely pleased at having the problem solved as he was. "So I can cancel the meeting with Production and Design?''

"Already took care of it. Bob and Frank are best buddies again, Purchasing is talking with Shoendorf about the problem, Bob shut down the assembly line until we run quality-control tests on all the boards in stock.... Crisis averted, thanks to you.''

Still laughing, Andie looked at his shirtfront and groaned. "I wish you'd put on a lab coat when you go down to the production floor to mess around. There's a clean shirt in your office.''

"Don't know what I'd do without you.'' Another quick kiss and he was on his feet, looking around to smile at Olivia. "Hello, Liv, darlin'. Here to take me to lunch?''

"Forget it,'' Andie spoke up promptly, her eyes glittering slightly. "We have to go over these figures again before this afternoon's meeting. Make it dinner, or reschedule.''

Olivia smiled, reaching up to brush a smudge off his cheek, her fingers lingering there for a moment. "She takes such good care of you, doesn't she?'' she said sweetly.

There was something in her voice, in the very air around them, that made Conn look first at her, then at Andie. Both smiled beatifically, as charming as cats on a windowsill.

And as deadly, Conn thought uneasily. There was something a little dangerous in Andie's eyes, and Olivia's red fingernails flashed slightly as she took her hand from his cheek.

Now what? He knew Andie didn't like Liv much, but there seemed to be an extra hint of hostility in the air today, a sense of something going on that he couldn't quite identify.

Not that he deluded himself into thinking he'd figure it out in this lifetime. The complexities and rituals of female politics had always baffled the hell out of him. He'd decided a long time ago that the smartest thing a man could do was keep his head down and his butt safely out of the line of fire.

"Come on in and I'll buy you a cup of coffee," he said easily, putting his hand on Liv's back and heading her gently but deliberately toward his office.

As the door closed behind them, he walked across to the hardwood table near the wall of windows overlooking Seattle's waterfront. The coffee carafe was almost full and he poured two cups of the special blend he had Starbucks make up for him. He handed one to Liv. "Cheers."

"More to the point, congratulations."

"For?"

Liv's mouth curved up in a gentle smile. "For finally getting rid of wife number two. It must feel nice, not having that hanging over you anymore."

"*Nice* isn't the word I would have chosen," Conn said quietly. He still hadn't entirely gotten used to the idea. He thought of Judith now deliberately, testing the memory for pain. Found only a weary sadness. "How did you find out? Don't tell me the press has hold of it already."

"A friend told a friend who told a friend who called me last night. I was going to drop by, but I had a dinner meeting that ran past midnight."

Conn thought of the bottle of Scotch still sitting on his kitchen counter. "Probably a good thing you didn't. I would have made lousy company."

"Oh, I'm sure I could have come up with an idea or two guaranteed to raise your spirits. And who knows what else...." She grinned salaciously. "Come on, Connor, lighten up! You look like the hero in a Gothic novel, all scowl and thunder."

He managed a rough smile. "It's probably just the hangover."

"Ahh." She gave a knowing smile. "I see. It was that way, was it?"

He grunted something vaguely affirmative and walked across the room to drop into one of the big armchairs by the window. He usually enjoyed sparring with Olivia, but he was tired today. The kind of tired that went bone-deep and made him feel as if he'd never shake free of it. "So, what can I do for you, Liv?"

"God, so formal." She kicked off her high heels and padded across to drop gracefully into the chair across from his. Lifting one long, curvaceous leg, she settled her bare foot into his lap. "You know why I'm here, Connor. I put a proposition to you a month ago. I'm still waiting for your answer."

Conn settled both hands around her small foot and started massaging it. "I didn't think you were serious, Liv."

"Deadly." She arched her foot, sighing in pleasure as he massaged her instep. "I want you to marry me. No strings, no fancy expectations, prenuptial agreements on both sides to protect our mutual business interests."

"We could just sleep together and save the lawyers' fees."

She laughed. "Hell, I've been trying to get you into my bed for eight months, Devlin, with nothing to show for it but a near-terminal case of frustration."

"I was married."

"You were separated. You and Judith hadn't lived together for almost a year when I first met you."

"Married is married," he said quietly. "It's like being pregnant, Liv—no halfways or almosts. I may not be able to make my marriages work, but I damned well won't sleep around while I *am* married."

She gave a small sigh of what might have been exasperation. "As you made abundantly clear the last time I flung myself at you, dear man. But the point is moot now. You are no longer married. That means you can do what the bunnies do, repeatedly and with enthusiasm. In fact, if I had the time, we could do it right here, right now."

Conn looked up at her uneasily, not knowing if she was teasing or not. You never quite knew with Olivia. But to his relief she didn't seem inclined to start flinging her clothes off, and he relaxed again. "I've been divorced about nineteen hours and a handful of minutes, Liv. Why in God's name would I be interested in getting married again?"

"Because I'm not Judith. Or Liza. I don't pretend to be in love with you, nor am I deluding myself into thinking you're in love with me. We're both wounded, both wary, both tired of the rubbish that comes with the marriage certificate. I've had two husbands in eight years, and each one told me he loved me and then, six months after the wedding, started trying to change me into the person he thought I should be."

She drew her foot from his grasp and tucked it under her, leaning forward slightly. "Connor, I'm thirty-four years old and I am one of the most successful corporate lawyers west of the Mississippi. I'm a workaholic, I don't have the inclination or the disposition to be the sweet corporate wife, and most of the eligible men I know couldn't handle my success, my temperament or my hours."

"And you think I can." He was intrigued in spite of himself.

"I know you can. You're as obsessed about your work as I am about mine, so the fact I spend most of my time in the office wouldn't bother you. And you're man enough that my success and money doesn't bother you."

She smiled. "You know as well as I do how cold it is out here in the big world of corporate success, Connor. I'd like to come home at night and have someone there, someone warm and uncomplicated. When I have a business or charity function to attend I'd like to go with a man I respect and admire, not the stud-of-the-week. I'm tired of playing the field. I like you. We seem to fit together pretty well. And I think it makes sense."

"Sort of the ultimate corporate merger."

"That's one way of looking at it."

"Pretty cold."

"You married for love twice, Connor," she said with quiet brutality. "Look what *it* got you."

There was no denying she had a point. Not with the ink still wet on his second divorce.

"And I want a baby." She said it with the impatience of someone face with a set of facts she can't quite believe. "If it wasn't for that, I'd agree to an affair. But my damned biological clock's ticking away like a time bomb. And, believe it or not, I'm just old-fashioned enough to believe a woman should be married to her baby's father." She smiled. "Sounds silly, doesn't it? You wouldn't think I'd give a damn."

"It sounds anything but silly," Conn told her quietly. Kids. He and Judith had fought day and night over kids. He'd wanted them, she hadn't and there had been no room for negotiation. "It'll be rough, raising a baby and keeping your career in the fast lane."

That had been Judith's problem with it, anyway, herself a businesswoman on the fast track.

"Rough, but not impossible. I can do it."

He had no doubt about it. "Is this a one-shot opportunity, or can I think about it for a few days?"

She laughed quietly. "I hardly expect you to jump into another marriage nineteen hours and a handful of minutes after your last one ended, Conn. Think about it. Take as long as you need—but don't take forever." Smiling, she slid to her feet and eased herself across his lap, straddling him. "Of course, I *could* give you an added incentive right now...if you've got a few minutes." Her hand glided playfully downward.

Conn caught her wrist firmly. "I thought you were in a hurry."

"I am. But I can be fast *and* good."

"A knack I've never mastered," he said calmly, turning his head to avoid her kiss. "I have a meeting in about five minutes, sweetheart, so don't get your engine revved too high."

"You're too young to be a stuffy old man, Connor. Five minutes is plenty of time to satisfy both parties involved if you get right down to business." She moved her pelvis suggestively.

"It takes me longer than five minutes just to figure out what tie to wear in the morning," Conn said with a laugh. "Cool down, Liv." Even if he weren't hung over, her offer held all the appeal of a hit-and-run accident.

To his relief she laughed good-naturedly, kissing his cheek lightly, then swung off his lap and straightened her jacket. "We would be good together, Conn. You know it and I know it. So think over what I said and get back to me."

She looked at her watch and frowned. "Damn, I'm late! I have a *major* meeting in less than an hour with the top honchos in a big investment firm. If I can convince them we can save them a few million in tax write-offs a year, their business will be worth a fortune. Wish me luck."

"You've got it." He got to his feet, suddenly distracted. Investments made him think of Alain DeRocher, which made him think of Andie, which made him think of her threat to marry and move to Montreal and have babies and play lacrosse and hockey or whatever the hell they did up there, leaving him and Devlin Electronics to fend for themselves. "And I'll, uh, call."

"Damn right you will, Devlin. Or I'll have your head on a platter." A quick peck on the cheek, then she was gone.

The door had barely closed behind her when it opened again and Conn glanced up, half expecting her to come flying back in to finish what she'd tried to start. But it was Andie, looking as cool and serene as always, although there was a glitter in her eyes that boded no good for anyone who got in her way.

"She says you're going to marry her."

Conn rubbed his forehead, squeezing his eyes closed for a moment. "The topic came up, yeah. But don't run out and buy us a wedding gift quite yet, darlin'. It ain't over 'til it's over."

"I've bought you two wedding gifts in the past eleven years," she said with an edge to her voice. "You don't get another."

Conn leaned well back in the soft armchair and looked at her. "Relax, Andie. I'm not marrying anyone, all right? Although, to quote a good friend of mine from just this morning, 'I don't know what you'd have to say about it if I did.'"

Her head lifted and she leveled a look at him that he'd seen bring strong men to their knees. "I think, as someone told *me* just this morning, that I have some right to know if you're going to marry that woman—" she bit the words out like poison "—for no other reason than twenty years of friendship."

Conn opened his mouth to deny it, then sighed, rubbing his forehead, wishing his head would stop pounding. "Hell, Andie, I've had worse offers. I married Liza because I thought I loved her, and I married Judith thinking I was in love with her. And right now I'm sitting here oh for two, thinking maybe—just *maybe*—that it's not the marrying part that gets me into trouble, but the being in love part. Maybe there is no such thing. Maybe you should just marry someone you don't hate too much, and take it from there."

Something crossed her face—a shadow, a hint of pain, gone in an instant. He looked at her curiously, expecting her to say something, but she just turned away and walked to the door. And as he watched the door close behind her, the thought hit him that if he had any sense at all he'd talk *her* into marrying him.

Although, he reminded himself as an afterthought, he couldn't marry his best friend. Because then she wouldn't be his best friend anymore, she'd be his wife. And then who would he turn to when the divorce came through?

Andie was still seething mad a couple of hours later.

Damn it, no one—*no* one—could be crazy enough to jump into one marriage while barely disentangled from the last one. And Conn Devlin was about the least crazy person she'd ever met.

Except when it came to women, she amended, fighting a surge of renewed fury. Heaven knows, she'd decided not long after he'd married Judith that it was a defective gene he had or something. Some sort of chemical imbalance that could turn a pragmatic and highly intelligent corporate shark into a complete idiot almost overnight.

Granted, he hadn't had a fighting chance with Judith. She'd zeroed in on him like a heat-seeking missile five minutes after she'd met him, and his fate had been sealed before he knew what had hit him.

Conn had been everything Judith had wanted in a husband. He was a self-made man, wealthy, well mannered and handsome as sin. He didn't slurp his soup or fumble with his cutlery; he wore a black tie like a fashion plate and could charm the frosty veneer off the most reserved dinner companion. He could choose a good wine, guide a sailboat, ride a horse, drive a fast car and handle a fast woman—and look damn good the whole while. On top of that, he knew people. Important people. And to a young and very ambitious businesswoman with the bit between her teeth, that was irresistible.

For her part, Judith was probably what Conn thought he wanted in a wife. Beautiful. Brilliant. Highly successful. They'd made a spectacular couple for the first year or so, slicing a swath through Seattle's upper crust that people still talked about. But then, little by little, the dream had started to tarnish.

Less than two years after he and Judith had been married, Conn had become withdrawn and uncommunicative and sullen-eyed, snapping at anyone who came too near, working crazy hours, shutting himself off. Andie had stayed out of it until New Year's Eve of that third year, when he'd turned up on her doorstep with no warning.

Telling her date to get the hell out, he'd poured himself a triple of brandy and had downed it in two long swallows;

then he'd flung the glass against the wall with a string of oaths that had made her stare at him in astonishment.

And then he'd told her about Judith. About the fight they'd had, again, over his desire to have children and her flat refusal to even discuss it. She'd married him, thinking he was as focused on the fast track as she was, only to discover that he was ready to relax a little, ready to enjoy some of the perks of success. Ready to start a family.

She was gone, he'd added tightly. She'd told him she was tired of it, tired of him. She was divorcing him.

In the following weeks, Conn's mood had gone from bad to worse. Then he'd shaken it off and had picked up the pieces of his life.

Except he'd been different afterward. Quieter. More introspective. Laughing less, spending more time alone. And a little colder, as though he'd shut off a part of himself and had no intention of ever letting anyone that close to him again.

Andie swore tiredly. If she had any sense, she'd go home. Pick up a salad from the deli for supper. Have a long soak in her big claw-footed bathtub, up to her neck in boiling hot water. Crawl into bed and just sleep until—

Her phone bleated and she reached for it wearily. "Yes?"

"Mr. Beck and his son are here, Andie."

"Here?" Andie sat straight up. "Now what!"

She shot to her feet, grabbing her suit jacket off the back of her chair and pulling it on as she hopped around on one foot, trying to get her shoes back on. She popped her head into Conn's office and told him, then, pausing long enough to run a comb through her hair and freshen her lipstick, she took a deep breath and walked out into the reception area.

Marc Beck saw her first. Grinning, he walked across and shook her hand warmly. "I nearly called you last night. A couple of symphony tickets fell into my lap at the last minute, and I remember you saying you like Chopin."

"I love Chopin." Andie smiled.

"Forget Chopin." Conn walked in just in time to catch Marc's offer, and as he strolled across to join the two of them, he found himself eyeing Marc speculatively. "Unless we can come to an agreement on this buy-out deal, you and I are still competitors in this business. And I'll consider any move you try making on my people as hostile." He smiled pleasantly enough as he said it, but there was a hint of very real irritation under the words.

Who the hell did this pup think he was, anyway, asking Andie for a date? Especially here, on Devlin turf.

Marc just grinned, seemingly unperturbed, his grip firm as he shook Conn's hand. "All the more incentive to get this deal hammered out and the money in the bank." He glanced at Andie, the smile warm. "I've always been partial to Chopin myself."

Conn had the sudden irrational urge to suggest that if he liked the damn music so much, why didn't he go home and listen to it instead of coming up here to hit on Andie? But he hung on to his temper, reminding himself that the deal with Becktron wasn't in the bag yet. And on top of that, he was already walking on thin ice as far as Andie was concerned.

So he simply smiled blandly instead. "Our meeting was set up for Friday. What's the problem?"

"That's one of reasons I like you so damn much, Devlin," a voice said from behind them. "You remind me of me. Straight to the point, and no wasted time."

Conn turned around just as Desmond Beck came through the wide glass doors from the outer corridor. He was built like a small building, not too tall but as solid as concrete, with thick gray hair and deceptively mild eyes and a ready smile.

Conn just nodded, waiting for it. Desmond Beck was a thorough, deliberate man, a brilliant engineer in his own right and a consummate businessman. Becktron had fallen on hard times in the past few years because of changes in the economy, not because of any mistakes its founder and president had made. Conn respected him probably more than anyone else in the industry.

Then, abruptly, the congenial smile vanished and those mild blue-gray eyes turned the color of cold steel. "I've gone over the last offer you presented, and I still have some questions about the actual implementation, Devlin."

"Then let's talk."

"I'll be honest with you, Devlin. Some of our people think we should shop Becktron around a bit. See what other offers we can get. Frankly, I've been wondering myself if it's just our patents you want. And if, after you get them, you'll just chop up the rest of the company and sell it off like old china at a garage sale."

"Your manufacturing facilities are outmoded," Conn said. "You survived on military contracts for years, but with the cutbacks in defense spending, you're halfway to bankruptcy, and we both know it. So let's stop dancing and get to the bottom line. Your patents are worth millions, and I'm willing to pay well for them."

He held Desmond's gaze. "But a lot of what I want doesn't have a price tag. Creativity. Genius. I want the brains behind your Research and Development. I want your engineers, your scientists, your programmers. What they know and what they can do. If Becktron goes down the tubes, these people will be on the street. I'm offering a good deal to those we take on, and fair compensation to those we don't."

He relaxed slightly, smiling. "Yes, I'm going to sell off what I don't need—outdated equipment, dead-end technology, some real estate. But everything that made Becktron what it is will still be intact."

Desmond gazed at Conn for a long, searching moment, then nodded abruptly. "Hell, you're right. I can't compete in today's world. Things are changing too fast. And if I have to sell, I'd just as soon it was to you. You've done in ten years what it took me close to thirty to accomplish, and you did it without cheating or losing your integrity, which is no small thing these days.''

"But some of Becktron's top-level management don't see it that way," Marc said quietly. "We dropped by today just to tell you we want to deal, but that we feel we need to do some more talking. There are all sorts of issues at stake here—not just the business end, but the employees. Pensions. Seniority.''

Conn fought his impatience. He wanted this deal tied up *now,* not sometime next week or the week after or—

Andie caught his eye just then and gave her head an almost inperceptible shake of warning, and Conn eased out a tight breath. The woman could read his mind like a Gypsy. Knew him better than he knew himself sometimes. He swallowed a grin and kept quiet.

"May I make a suggestion?" Andie looked at Beck thoughtfully. "The concerns you've brought up today are valid and negotiable—it's just a matter of getting the numbers right. What you and Conn need to do to finalize this deal is to simply sit down somewhere quiet where you can talk—am I right?"

Desmond smiled. "I'm certainly willing."

Conn fought a surge of satisfaction, keeping his expression blank, smart enough to stay the hell out of the way while Andie worked her magic.

"Then I suggest we all go up to Timberwolf Lodge for a few days and settle things once and for all. We can book the entire lodge for ourselves. It's quiet and secluded and has all the amenities, plus full conference facilities.''

Desmond looked at her in surprise. "That," he said after a thoughtful moment, "is a damned good idea. Marc?"

His son nodded, looking impressed. "Perfect. We've all been running in circles with this thing for weeks and everyone's tired. One last round of discussions, one on one, just might wrap it all up.''

"Do it." Desmond looked at his watch. "I have to go. Set things up, talk with Marc about anything you need, let me know when and where. I'll be there with my people."

"Sounds great." Marc smiled down at Andie. "Maybe we'll get a chance to spend some time talking about something *other* than business while we're up there."

Andie's smile widened. "That would be—"

"Unlikely," Conn said shortly, not liking the way Beck was standing so damned close to her. Not liking the way he was still holding her hand after shaking it, either. Not liking anything at all about the man, as a matter of fact. Not his smile, the cut of his clothes, the way he carried himself—none of it. "We've got a lot of details left to work out. I doubt we're going to have much time for socializing."

Andie gave him an unfathomable look, but Conn ignored her. And finally, after another round of handshaking and smiles—too damn much of each in Marc Beck's case, to Conn's way of thinking—the two men left.

Conn headed back through Andie's office to his own, unsettled and irritable for some reason, thinking about the way Andie had been looking at Beck. Almost as though she actually liked the jerk, Conn thought in annoyance. As though she couldn't see through the high-priced suit and expensive haircut to the spoiled rich man's kid underneath.

"Well, that certainly was interesting." Andie followed him into his office, closing the door behind her and walking across to help herself to a cup of coffee.

"Yeah." Conn dropped into his leather chair and leaned back, looking around at her. "That was a good idea you had out there, taking negotiations up to Timberwolf."

"I wasn't talking about Becktron, I was talking about the way you cut Marc Beck off at the knees out there." She strolled around to the front of his desk, a cup of steaming coffee in her hand. "You have a problem with him or something?"

"The kid's a jerk," Conn muttered, reaching up to loosen his tie.

"Kid?" Andie's voice was filled with laughter. "He's the same age you are, Connor."

"In years, maybe. But you know what they say, honey— it ain't the years, it's the mileage."

"Mmm." She nodded, still watching him with that slightly thoughtful expression. "Competition making you a little jumpy?"

"Competition?" Conn gave a snort. "I'm buying Becktron out from under him, aren't I? If he had what it took, he'd have found a way to bail his old man out without having to sell off the business."

"That's not the kind of competition I was talking about. Although last week you told me that selling off Becktron before it bankrupted them was the smartest thing the Becks could do."

"That was last week," Conn growled.

"And Marc's computer company? Last week you said that new design he's come up with is going to set the entire industry on its ear."

"Like I said, that was last week." Conn pulled a stack of papers toward him, then shoved it away again. "What's with you and this guy, anyway?" He gave her a jaundiced look. "Funny, I never heard you say anything about liking Chopin before." He drew out the composer's name sarcastically.

"Why would I?" Andie's eyes flashed. "Your idea of classical music is Jimi Hendrix setting his guitar on fire."

"Since when did you get to be such a music snob? I've been in the car with you when you roll the top down and the stereo up as we go belting down I-5 with Billy Idol's 'L.A. Woman' cranked up to about five hundred decibels."

"I thought you liked Billy Idol," she said indignantly.

"The question is, does Marc Beck like him?"

Andie stared at him for a full beat. "And just what is that supposed to mean?"

Conn had his mouth half open to tell her exactly what it meant, then realized he didn't know himself. "Nothing," he muttered, running his fingers through his hair. "Hell, Andie, it didn't mean anything—all right? I'm just hung over and tired, and this whole Becktron deal's got me wired tighter than a three-dollar radio. I thought we had everything going smooth as silk, and now I'm not so sure."

Andie eyed him mistrustfully for another moment or two, then finally she nodded, relaxing. "It's going to be all right, Conn. Beck just wants to get all the loose ends tied off, that's all."

"Damn it, they're practically bankrupt! This is the best deal he'll ever get—he knows that. Anyone else will grab his company's patents and sell off the rest at garage-sale prices, union contracts, pension funds and seniority be damned."

Andie had to smile, hearing the frustration in Conn's voice. "Relax. He's just getting prenuptial jitters. Becktron is his life, like Devlin Electronics is yours. He's worried about his people. He wants to make sure they're taken care of, that's all."

"I said I'll take care of them, damn it," Conn said angrily. "What the hell does he want from me, blood?"

"Your time. Your reassurance."

Conn gave a thoughtful grunt. Then, almost grudgingly, he smiled, running his fingers through his already-tousled hair again. "You're right, as always. Tell Timberwolf I want computer and fax hookups, photocopy access, meeting rooms—the works. Minimal staff only. And tell them if they let anything slip to the press, I'll buy them out and turn them into a monkery."

"I think the term is monastery."

"Whatever." He flashed her a quick grin. "Hell, considering the shape my sex life is in, I'm a first-rate candidate for the place myself."

"I'm sure Olivia will be only too glad to take care of that for you," Andie said sweetly. Just the thought of Olivia Woodruff in bed with Conn made her blood boil, but she smiled determinedly and pushed her chair back, getting to her feet. "I'll call Timberwolf and set things up."

"Hey!" Conn reached out and caught her by the arm as she went to walk by him. Leaning back in his leather armchair, he let her arm slide through his grasp until he was holding her hand, fingers meshed with hers. "There's nothing between Olivia Woodruff and me, all right? Yeah, we've gone out a few times. And yeah, she made me an offer this morning most men would give their right arm for. But I'm not interested."

Andie smiled carelessly, praying he couldn't read anything in her eyes. He knew her so damned well, it was hard to hide anything from him, yet at times it was as though he didn't know her at all. "I'm not your keeper, Conn," she reminded him with an offhand smile. "You don't have to tell me your plans."

"I know I don't," he said with a hint of impatience. "But this thing with Olivia seems to be sticking in your craw for some reason, and I just want to put your mind at ease. I'm not in love with her, I'm not going to marry her, I'm not going to marry anyone." A grin flickered across his mouth. "I'd rather marry you. What do you say we run off to Tahoe for the weekend and get hitched and spend a few days in bed and—"

"You should be so lucky," she said with a reckless laugh, bending down to kiss him on the cheek just so he couldn't see her eyes.

Conn turned his head at the last instant and to her surprise Andie found herself kissing him on the mouth instead, his lips surprisingly soft against hers. It was so unexpected that she didn't pull away, slightly off balance, and in the next heartbeat he turned his head ever so slightly to settle his mouth more firmly against hers and then was kissing her with satisfactory thoroughness.

Senses scattered, breathless, a little dizzy, Andie put her hand on his shoulder, intending to push herself free of him. But then his lips parted with silken insistence and she started kissing him back without really thinking about it, welcoming the sly touch of his tongue, feeling herself start to slip dangerously near the edge of self-control.

The phone bleated loudly and Andie tore her mouth from Conn's, heart racing, flustered and out of breath. Shaking her fingers free of his grasp, she turned and grabbed the receiver. "What?"

There was a startled silence on the other end, then Margie's voice, slightly reproachful. "It's Frank Czarnecki for Connor, Andie. Something about the DeepSix project. Do you want me to have him call back?"

"No." Stepping well away from Conn, she took a deep breath. "No, he'll take it. Thanks." Still holding the receiver, she stood there for an unsteady moment, not even daring to look at Conn. "It's Frank. About DeepSix."

He reached up to take the receiver from her hand, looking at her, a tiny frown wedged between his strong brows. "We, uh, maybe we should talk about this."

Taking another deep breath, she slipped from between him and his desk. "DeepSix is your baby," she said carelessly, deliberately misunderstanding him. "Right now I've got to talk with Timberwolf."

"Not DeepSix, damn it, Andie!"

He looked perplexed and a little unsettled, and suddenly Andie didn't want to talk to him about anything, least of all why she'd been kissing him as though she meant it. This morning's lapse in the kitchen had been one thing—he'd come on to her, after all, so she could blame her reactions on surprise and sleep deprivation. But this slip had been all hers. And there was no way she could explain what the *hell* she'd been doing without making things even worse than they already were.

Before he could say anything more, she reached across and pressed a button on his phone, bringing Frank Czarnecki on-line; then she turned and headed for the door as though she had nothing on her mind at all but the upcoming negotiations with Becktron.

Conn had his mouth open to call her back, then realized Czarnecki was on the other end of the receiver, no doubt wondering what the hell was going on. Swallowing his impatience and confusion, he ran his fingers through his hair, then loosened the knot in his tie and undid the collar button on his shirt. "Frank. What can I do for you?"

Something was going on, and he didn't like it one damned bit.

Conn wandered across his wide, dimly lit living room again and stood by the windows, looking down at the wide expanse of lawn through the light drizzle that coated everything in gray.

And as he had about twenty times tonight, he glanced around at the phone on the elegant fruitwood writing desk against the far wall. He wanted to call her. Wanted her to come over, filling the rooms around him with that special warmth and good humor she carried with her like sunshine. And he wanted to touch her again. To fill his hands with her silken mane of hair and run it through his fingers and lower his mouth to hers and kiss her until he was dizzy with it.

And *that* was what was keeping him from picking up the phone and dialing her number.

He lifted the half-forgotten mug of coffee in his hand and took a swallow, barely tasting it. Because the woman he was thinking about as he might a lover wasn't Olivia Woodruff or any of a dozen other beautiful and all-too-willing women he could think of, but Andie Spencer.

Those few erotic minutes with her that morning had triggered an attack of the wants so bad, he could taste it. And while his brain knew that making love to Andie was out of the question, his body had no such qualms.

He glowered out into the misty night and thought, idly, of calling Olivia. She'd be all too happy to come over and take the edge off.

Except that was just a little too clinical. Granted, he'd pretty much given up on the concept of *love*, but there should still be more to a sexual encounter than simple physical release. Hell, if that's all he wanted, he didn't need Olivia *or* Andie.

It made him smile slightly and he met his own gaze on the rain-wet window. Divorce blues, Andie had called it. That's all this was.

He glanced at the phone again, wanting to call Andie. Knowing he didn't dare. And wondering what this strange empty wanting was that sat cold and low in his belly.

Four

────

When the phone rang a little after three, Andie simply groaned and pulled the covers over her head. Not this time. No way. He could plead and beg all he wanted, but she was *not* running over there again, divorce blues or no.

The phone chimed insistently again, and she swore with more heat than imagination and struggled free of the covers, squinting at the clock as though to assure herself it really was three in the morning.

It was.

Grabbing the receiver, she shoved it against her ear. "This," she snarled sleepily, "had better be damned good!"

The sizzle of an empty line answered her. Then, quietly, a voice murmured, "Oh, damn! I forgot the time change, sweetheart. Did I wake you?" A soft chuckle. "Come to think of it, I hope I did, considering it's what . . . two in the morning over there?"

"Three," she mumbled, sinking back against the mound of pillows, eyes closed. "Alain! Where on earth are you?"

"Paris, darling. Didn't you get my message?"

"Message?" Andie rubbed her eyes with her knuckles, vaguely remembering seeing something on her desk about Paris. "Um, yeah. Yeah, I did, I guess. Forgot, that's all."

"I'd hoped you might call tonight," he chided gently. "I gave Margie the number."

"Sorry—I've been run off my feet all day. I got home late and just crashed."

"Bad news. I'm stuck here for another week, at least. I know I promised to come out to the coast this weekend, but..."

She could hear the shrug in his voice and winced guiltily. She'd completely forgotten he'd been planning to come out to Seattle this weekend. "That's... um... actually just as well. Conn's negotiating to buy out a major competitor, and I'm working crazy hours. We're going to be tied up all weekend."

"You and Connor? Together?"

She smiled into the darkness. "Along with a dozen or so other people."

Alain gave a grunt. "So let that dozen or so other people take care of things, and fly over here in the morning. You can shop and go sightseeing while I'm in my meetings, and we can spend the evenings together, drinking wine and playing tourist."

Andie laughed. "It's tempting, but..."

"But Conn wins again," he said with a hint of irritation in his voice.

"This isn't a contest, Alain," Andie said quietly.

She could almost hear him smile. "No, I know it's not, sweetheart. Sorry. It's just that I miss you. And it bugs the hell out of me that I'm stuck in the most romantic city in the world—alone—while Connor Devlin's got you all to himself."

"He's just a friend, Alain. You know that."

"So you keep saying. But the way you talk about him, I sometimes wonder."

"Well, you don't have to worry." Andie stared at the ceiling. Thinking of Conn. Wishing . . . well, just wishing.

"You sound sad."

"Tired." Andie gave herself a slight shake. "Just tired."

He gave a rueful laugh. "My fault. I've been so busy, I lose track of time. It's just that after four solid days of talking bottom lines and investment rates and stock options, I was desperate to hear your voice."

"I'm glad you called."

"I wish I were there with you right now. Are you wearing that pale blue negligee I gave you for your birthday?"

"Of course." She'd never taken the gift out of the elegant silver box it had come in, but it was just a small lie. "I think of you every time I put it on." Another lie. She realized, with a faint sense of shame, that she rarely thought of Alain at all.

"If I was there with you, you wouldn't be wearing anything." His voice wrapped around her like silk. "If I close my eyes I can feel your skin, taste your mouth. . . ."

"I . . . um . . . It's awfully late, Alain. I have to be up and reasonably alert in another four hours. Maybe you can call back tomorrow evening and we can talk about it then?"

He was silent for a long moment, then he chuckled. "You're probably right. I should keep my mind on business. But before I go, there's something we need to talk about."

Andie braced herself instinctively, fingers tightening around the receiver.

"I know I said I wouldn't push you, Andie, but if we *are* going to get married this fall, we have to start making some plans. My mother's already got herself tied in knots, and we haven't even set a date."

Andie bit her lower lip, wishing she could just say yes and mean it. That she could truly love Alain as easily as he seemed to have fallen in love with her. That she could just accept all he had to offer and be happy.

Knowing it was never going to be that easy at all.

"Yes," she said very quietly. "I know. But I..." She swallowed a sigh. "I need more time, Alain. Not just getting married, but all of it—quitting my job, leaving my family and friends and—" And Conn, she almost said. I'd have to leave Conn.

Instead, she just squeezed her eyes closed and fought back the sudden surge of emotion. "I'm sorry. I'm not making sense, I know. And it's not fair to you to..."

"It's all right, sweetheart," he murmured. "I understand. Just don't say no. Not yet. Think about it. Take as much time as you need. I'll be here for you."

"Oh, Alain..." The tears caught her so by surprise that two of them rolled down her cheeks before she could even blink. "I'm handling this badly. Thank you for being so patient with me."

"Look, honey, I have to run. The next meeting is starting. Give me a call tomorrow sometime, all right? I'll be in meetings all day, but tell my secretary to page me. Now go back to sleep."

"I will. And, Alain—"

"Good night, darling. I love you."

The receiver went down gently in Paris, and Andie lay there and listened to the dial tone for a long while, her throat aching with tears. Damn it, it *should* be so simple! Most women would kill to be in her shoes, being wooed by one of the world's most eligible bachelors. He was handsome and charming and sweet, had a town house in Quebec City and a two-hundred-year-old château in the country and he loved her. So why in heaven's name couldn't she just be in love with *him* instead of with Conn, who wasn't in love with anyone?

"Five days? You're going to be staying at a romantic mountain resort with Connor Devlin for five days?" Andie's younger sister gave a whoop. "Well, that's more like it! Maybe old Conn's got a brain cell or two that's still

functioning after all!'' She gave a dirty-sounding chuckle.
"With luck, that's not all that's functioning."

"Work, Tracy—we're going up there to *work.*"

"Mmm. Speaking of Connor Devlin, how many men does it take to change a light bulb?"

Andie closed her eyes, waiting for it. "How many?"

"One. He just stands there and holds the bulb, and waits for the world to revolve around him."

Andie had to laugh. "And you think that's Conn?"

Tracy looked thoughtful. "Not really. He's so focused on Devlin Electronics, I don't think he's even *aware* of the world half the time. That's the only reason I can think of why he can *look* at you for twenty-some years, and still not *see* you."

Andie just smiled. Then she frowned and looked at the open suitcase on her bed, then at her closet. "I'm forgetting something. . . ."

"That knock-your-eyes-out blue silk negligee that what's-his-name gave you," Tracy said firmly. "God knows, it's not as though you're wearing it for *him.* So drag it out and put it to work, big sister."

"I will not!" Andie turned to glare at her sister, who was sprawled comfortably across the end of her bed. "Trust me, Tracy, this weekend is going to be as romantic as a case of poison ivy."

"Well, for heaven's sake, you can *change* that easily enough!" Tracy sat up, gesturing impatiently. "He's divorced now, Andie, remember? Unattached. Up for grabs. So pack that suitcase full of your sexiest clothes, a gallon or so of expensive perfume and a couple of those lift-'em-up-and-shove-'em-out bras for a little old-fashioned cleavage, and let nature take its course!"

Andie gave Tracy a long-suffering look. "I know this is a difficult concept for you to grasp, Tracy, but when I say I'm going to be working up at Timberwolf, I mean just that—meetings and more meetings. If I go up there parading around in perfume and cleavage, Conn will think I've flipped out and he'll have me locked away. Permanently.''

"How much longer are you going to moon over this guy, Andie?" Tracy wasn't smiling now. "You're nearly thirty, in case it's slipped your attention."

"It hasn't, thanks."

"And what about your Frenchman?"

"He's Canadian. And what about him?" Andie gathered up a handful of lingerie and stuffed it into the suitcase.

"Are you going to marry him, or what?" Tracy got to her feet and wandered over to Andie's dresser, starting to poke through the drawers. She found a black lacy uplift bra and tossed it into the suitcase, following it with the matching lace briefs.

Andie grabbed them up and put them back into the drawer. "I haven't made up my mind yet."

"Time's a-passing." Tracy found another lacy bra, this one in pale pink, and she tossed it into the suitcase. "I can't believe you're not even sleeping with him. You might be nearly thirty, but you're not ready to go on the shelf yet. Heck, I was reading an article in a magazine last week that said you can still do it right into your eighties."

"I feel *so* much better knowing that." Andie shoved the pink bra back into the drawer, slapped Tracy's hands out of the way and slammed it closed. "And there *are* more important things in life than sex, believe it or not."

"Quick, name three!" Laughing out loud, Tracy wandered across to the closet and started looking through the things hanging there. A black cocktail dress caught her attention and she took it out and held it against herself, then tossed it into the suitcase. "You should at least be sleeping with the guy, Andie. It's not as though Connor's saving his lily-white body for *you*. You said he and Olivia Woodruff are an item?" She glanced around at Andie, eyebrow raised. "I've heard about her."

Andie put the dress back in the closet just as Tracy was pulling out a two-piece knit outfit, eyeing the deep V-neck speculatively. Snatching it out of Tracy's hand, she returned it to the closet, too. "I know you have a single-track mind, but it's not what you think. Conn has this old-fashioned sense of propriety that keeps him from sleeping with one woman while he's married to another."

"But he's not married anymore, is he?"

That same thought had occurred to Andie, but she didn't want to think about it now. "I work for Conn, I don't run his life for him."

"But you're still in love with him." Tracy looked at her.

Andie avoided her sister's gaze, suddenly busy choosing which shoes to pack. "He's my best friend. Of course I love him. I love you, too, although there are days I wonder why."

Tracy started to say something, then thought better of it and sighed instead, taking the black cocktail dress out of the closet again and putting it back in the suitcase. "You'll need this. Timberwolf Lodge isn't the kind of place where you wear jeans and a sweatshirt to dinner."

"We're going to be the only people up there, so I imagine we can go to dinner stark naked if we want." But Andie did leave the dress in the suitcase.

"Now there's an idea," Tracy said with a sly grin. "I'll bet even Conn would sit up and take notice if you—"

"Forget it."

"Perfume. Don't forget your perfume. Oh, and here— take these." Tracy had her handbag in her lap and was digging something out of her makeup case. "With luck, you'll even get a chance to use them." Grinning broadly, she reached over and tossed a couple of individually wrapped condoms into the middle of the suitcase.

"Good grief, would you stop it!" Andie snatched them up and dropped them back into Tracy's open purse. "And for heaven's sake don't let Dad know you carry those around or he'll lock you in the basement. His definition of safe sex is no sex."

"The kind you're practicing, you mean." Tracy's grin was filled with devilry as she pulled open another drawer in the dresser and started pulling out Andie's collection of night-wear. "Jeez, I don't believe this!" She held up a plain white cotton nightgown. "Nuns wear racier stuff than this, An-die! Honestly, you and I have to have a *serious* talk about your love life!"

"Damn it, Tracy, would you please get out of—"

"Aha, what's this?" She rooted through the drawer, eyes narrowed, and came up with a triumphant grin, a froth of apricot chiffon in her hand. "Now *this* is more like it! Ooh la la." She held it up to herself and gave a sexy pirouette. "Another gift from the Frenchman?"

"A gift from myself." Andie reached across to take it from her, but Tracy snatched it away.

"Well, maybe you're not entirely hopeless after all," she said with a chuckle, folding it neatly and setting it in the suitcase. "Take it with you. Old Conn won't know what hit him."

"Neither will you if you don't stop messing around."

"You still haven't told me if you're going to marry Alain."

"I did tell you. I said I haven't made up my mind yet."

"But you're thinking about it."

"Now and again." She said it lightly, not wanting to dis-cuss Alain. Or marriage. Or Conn Devlin, either, for that matter. "I'd love another cup of coffee—how about you?"

"Do it, Andie," Tracy said quietly, suddenly serious. She reached out and grasped Andie's hand. "It's time you got over Conn, Andie. Alain loves you. Grab that and be happy."

"Condoms, fashion advice and premarital counseling." Andie laughed carelessly, not feeling like laughing at all. Everything Tracy said was true, but she didn't want to hear it. "I think you're missing your calling, studying anthro-pology. If digging up old pots loses its charm, you have a bright future as an advice columnist. Or a talk-show host."

"And you've got a bright future as an old maid unless you get as practical and down-to-earth about Conn as you are about everything else in your life," Tracy shot back, only half joking. "You are the most together woman I know, Andie. You've got your whole life under control except where Connor Devlin's concerned. And it's—"

"Off-limits," Andie said quietly. "Don't push it, Tracy."

Tracy paused, mouth still open, obviously brimming over with good advice she was dying to share. Then, wisely, she shut it and nodded, smiling good-naturedly. "Sorry."

Andie had to laugh, reaching out to ruffle Tracy's mop of hair. "You're forgiven. And you said you were going to bring back the camera I lent you six months ago, remember?"

"It's in the car—I'll bring it in while you finish packing." She grinned, heading for the door. "And take that sexy nightie, big sister. You just never know...."

Timberwolf Lodge was set high up in the Cascades, a major ski resort that in the off-season specialized in hosting getaway business conferences and workshops. It was about a three-hour drive from Seattle, but it was going to take them closer to five, Conn figured.

He was in no rush to get there. It was a beautiful morning, the air like crystal, the sky the color of wedgewood, without a cloud to mar it. The kind of morning he all-too-rarely stopped to enjoy. But he was damned well going to enjoy this one.

He'd picked Andie up a little after seven that morning and he was deliberately taking his time, stopping at every lookout, pulling over at one point to watch three deer graze on a nearby hillside. They picked up a couple of soft drinks and some grapes at a roadside market and then, a few miles later, pulled off at a picnic table by a small lake and ate them in the late-morning sunshine, laughing and chatting about this and that.

It had been too long since he'd done this sort of thing, Conn thought as the road wound ever higher and the mountains started to close in around them. The past ten years had been good ones, but they'd taken their toll. Two marriages, among other things.

Frowning, he guided his mind away from that topic as skillfully as he guided his Jeep around a tight hairpin curve. The air was spicy with the scent of pine and he took a deep breath of it, feeling some of the tightness across his shoulders fall away, realizing he was honestly looking forward to the next few days. Not just the prospect of getting the Becktron deal wrapped up, but just being out of the city.

He glanced at Andie. She had her eyes closed and looked relaxed and happy, chestnut hair whipping around in the wind coming through the Jeep windows, one foot braced on the gear console, the other long leg stretched out comfortably.

Conn's gaze was drawn to those smooth, tanned legs again and again, and he wondered idly how long it had been since he'd seen her in shorts. Daring to take his eyes off the winding road, he gave the rest of her a thoughtful glance. Her bare arms and shoulders were sun-browned, too, as was the sweep of skin above the simple top she was wearing, and he found himself thinking a little irritably that it looked like a sailing tan.

Did that French-Canadian she was dating take her sailing? he wondered. There'd once been a time when *he'd* taken her sailing, but he never seemed to be able to fit it in anymore. Judith had hated the boat, had hated being taken away from her work, and although he'd gone out by himself a few times, it just hadn't been the same.

And he missed it, he realized suddenly. Missed the sailing, and missed Andie. She was his best friend, yet they hardly spent time together. Maybe it was time to change that.

If she didn't marry that damned DeRocher, of course. He was beginning to wish he'd never introduced the two of them in the first place.

Impulsively, he reached across and covered one of Andie's hands with his, meshing their fingers. She opened her eyes and looked at him questioningly, and Conn just smiled. "Kind of feels like old times, doesn't it? It's been a long while since we spent a weekend together."

Andie smiled dryly. "If you'd quit getting married, maybe we could fit it in. But your wives have never liked the idea of your spending time with your administrative assistant."

To his surprise, it made Conn laugh. "Liza always did think you and I had something going. And Judith..." He shrugged. "Well, Judith probably wouldn't have minded if we had, as long as it got me out of her hair so she could get some work done."

Andie's fingers tightened slightly on his, and Conn smiled slightly. "In a way, I probably deserved it. What goes around comes around."

"Playing second fiddle to Judith's career?"

"Like Liza played second fiddle to mine," he said quietly. The road took a sharp right turn and Conn had to let go of Andie's hand to downshift. But she didn't draw it back into her lap, and after he'd brought the Jeep through the curve and had shifted back into third, he reached down and braided his fingers with hers again.

"She married me, figuring she was getting the perfect husband. Billy Soames and I had beat the odds and the company was going strong, I'd just bought the house, things looked great."

"Every coed's dream," Andie muttered beside him.

Conn smiled. Andie had never liked Liza. And in spite of his best efforts, the feeling had been mutual.

"Then you and Billy disagreed about the business risks you were willing to take," she said. "You bought him out and put Devlin Electronics into high gear and suddenly Liza had an absentee husband who worked, ate and slept work.''

"You can't blame her for being pretty choked up. Hell, she was still in college. Everyone was still partying 'til dawn, going skiing, having a good time. Except us. I was working twenty-hour days, didn't even have time to talk to her half the time let alone take her to parties. She was stuck out in that huge house by herself.''

"She knew what she was getting into," Andie said with quiet intensity. "If she'd paid any attention to what you were doing, she'd have known you can't just—"

"No excuses, darlin'," Conn said with a soft laugh. "It was my fault the marriage failed—there's no getting around it. She wanted kids right away, I didn't. She wanted a normal life with a husband who was around, and I couldn't give it to her. When she met Richard and divorced me, it was the smartest thing she could have done. For both of us."

He managed a rough smile. "Ironic that one of the reasons Judith left me was because I wanted kids and she didn't. That I was ready to settle down and start taking things easy and her career was just starting to take off."

"Yeah, you do seem to have trouble getting it right, Devlin." Andie let her head fall back against the headrest and turned to look at him, letting her gaze follow the familiar contours of his strong profile.

She could still see the faint scar running along the angle of his jaw where he'd nearly killed himself twenty years ago, falling off old man Hennigan's garage roof into a pile of scrap lumber. She'd thought he *had* killed himself that afternoon, looking down off the edge of the roof and seeing him lying there, pale and still, covered with blood.

She could still remember how sick with terror she'd been, how great, even then, the sense of loss. She'd nearly broken her own neck scrambling down off the roof. By the time she'd fought her way over the fence and through the blackberry brambles to where he'd fallen, he'd managed to sit up, dazed and still bleeding.

He'd reached for her instinctively and she'd been there for him, clutching him against her, sticky with blood, then, finally, screaming at the top of her lungs, terrified to leave his side. Hennigan and two other neighbors had come running; someone had called the ambulance, someone else had called his parents.

An afternoon in the hospital and fifteen stitches later, he was home, grinning that cocky thirteen-year-old grin, showing off the bandages like a war hero, basking in the awe-filled adulation of his peers.

But that day had marked a change in their relationship. Until then, they'd been next-door buddies, getting in and out of scrapes, sharing adventures and comic books and the occasional soft drink. But from that afternoon on, there had been something special between them, something strong and private that excluded everyone else.

A few days later, Conn had taken her out into the garage and had rummaged through his father's toolbox until he'd found the hunting knife. Solemnly, he'd made a deep cut first on his thumb, then on hers. They'd held them together and had sworn a blood-brother oath to always be there for each other, to always be best friends.

Smiling, Andie ran her finger down the scar on her thumb. Blood brothers.

They pulled up into the parking lot at Timberwolf a little before noon, and Conn was pleased to notice that the others were already there. Margie's little red car was parked next to Bob Miller's sedan, and Frank Czarnecki's muddy old truck sat off to one side. There were a couple of other cars there he didn't recognize—Beck's people, probably.

Beck and his son were coming in by helicopter later that afternoon. Conn had thought of flying in himself at one point, but he was glad now he hadn't. He felt rested and relaxed and ready for battle, and he found himself grinning for no particular reason as he carried his garment bag and Andie's small suitcase up the wide stone steps.

The big carved pine doors were standing open to the morning's warmth, and as he waited for Andie to go through, he looked around with satisfaction. Perfect. With the ski runs closed and the summer season not yet open, things were dead quiet. Perfect for the kind of intense negotiations ahead.

Conn's grin widened as he followed Andie across the massive great room to the desk, enjoying the silken flash of her long tanned legs in the sunlight filtering through the acres of glass arching up and across the far end of the lodge. No doubt about the scenery being pretty damn good.

Not that Andie's legs were the only gorgeous thing in the place. The cathedral ceiling rose twenty feet above them, crisscrossed with massive timber rafters. Racks of elk and deer antlers hung here and there along the walls, and under them were hundreds of framed photographs documenting the history of the lumber industry in the area. A massive fieldstone fireplace and hearth took up almost one end wall and groupings of comfortable furniture sat around big braided rag rugs that lay like bright pools on the golden pine floor.

The manager greeted them both energetically, said the others were out on the big flagstone terrace having lunch, and then gave them their keys and pointed them toward the wide split-log stairs leading upstairs.

They had the two end suites, and Conn followed Andie into hers and put her bag down, looking around approvingly. "This'll do fine." He nodded toward the door connecting this suite with his own. "Mind if I open that? When the going gets hot and heavy, it'll make things easier."

Andie glanced at the door, having to smile. "Sure, as long as you think you can control yourself."

He just looked at her blankly.

Andie rolled her eyes with mock exasperation. "Thanks a lot, Devlin! When the going gets hot and heavy—get it? You're supposed to say that it'll be difficult as hell controlling yourself, having a beautiful, naked woman sleeping just steps away. Most bosses would think they'd died and gone to heaven, having an opportunity to sneak into their assistant's bedroom at midnight for a little hanky-panky.''

Conn gave her such an odd look that Andie had to laugh out loud. ''Joke, Devlin,'' she said, still laughing. ''It was just a joke! Of course you can open it. I'm sure I'll be quite safe.''

If she had any sense, *she'd* sneak into *his* room at midnight and see what trouble *she* could stir up.

Conn was still frowning, as though not too certain he really got the joke, but he unlocked the door after a moment or two and walked through to his own side in thoughtful silence. And Andie, watching him, didn't know whether to throw something or just laugh.

Five

A beautiful, naked woman sleeping just steps away...

Swearing under his breath, Conn rolled onto his back, kicking his feet free of the sheets, and glowered at the ceiling.

If only she knew. If she had *any* idea of the fantasies that had been taunting him these past couple of days, of the thoughts that had been slithering around in the darker corners of his mind. Bad thoughts. Dark thoughts. Thoughts that no decent man had about his best friend...

A beautiful, naked woman sleeping just steps away...

The image wouldn't leave him. Every time he closed his eyes, he could see her in there, lying between the crisp cotton sheets in that massive king-size bed.

Beautiful. Naked.

Damn.

The big bedroom was flooded with moonlight, and he turned his head to look at the window, thinking he should get up and pull the drapes closed. He could see the rounded flank of Wolf Mountain rising against the pale, star-speckled sky, and he lay staring at it, wishing he knew what the hell was wrong with him.

He'd thought at first that it was just those divorce blues Andie had teased him about. Them, and a bad case of lust.

But he was starting to wonder. Maybe the problem wasn't that simple. Maybe the problem was *him*.

And then there was Marc Beck.

In spite of himself, Conn felt his hands curl into fists. Now there was a *major* problem in the making.

Desmond Beck and his son and a couple of Becktron bean counters had flown in sometime that afternoon, and it had taken Conn all of five seconds to recognize he was going to have trouble.

Not with the Becktron buy-out—Desmond had come up here wanting to sell. All they had to do was hammer out the details.

No, the trouble was going to be with Marc.

He'd stepped off that damned helicopter like a hero coming home from the war, hair flying in the wind, teeth glinting in an easy grin. Spotting Andie, he'd come striding across the helipad toward her. And then—

Conn gritted his teeth. *Then* the bastard had kissed her.

Kissed her. Right on the mouth. Right there, in front of everyone. And Andie, damn it, hadn't even seemed to mind.

In fact, Conn thought sourly, no one had seemed to pay much attention to it except him. Was he the *only* person up here Beck hadn't conned? The only person who could see what was going on?

And if it wasn't bad enough he had to worry about Beck single-handedly, now he had to contend with his own unruly libido.

He'd been lying here for hours in the dark, thinking about her. Thinking about her lying in bed. Thinking about her lying in bed naked. Thinking about what it would be like to go in there and slip between the sheets with her and draw her against him and—

Conn groaned out loud and sat up, rubbing his stubbled face with his hands. This had to stop. He was a grown man, for crying out loud, not a randy teenager. And Andie, hell, Andie wasn't that kind of woman. Andie was . . . Andie.

Unsettled and wide-awake now, he got up and walked into the bathroom to splash cold water on his face. He thought a cold shower probably wouldn't have been a bad idea, either.

He wandered back through the bedroom and stood at the French doors opening out onto the big deck. He'd left one of them slightly ajar and he pushed it open and walked outside, the cold mountain air caressing his naked skin more sensually than he'd have thought possible.

The icy night air should have cooled him off in more ways than one, but standing there naked in the moonlight seemed to have the opposite effect and he felt himself becoming even more aroused. Teeth gritted, he prowled the deck, as restless as a cat, pausing in the deep shadows on the far side for a moment. He found himself looking at the five-foot gap between his deck and Andie's. The double French doors leading into her bedroom stood half open and he fantasized for a split second about—

She appeared in the doorway as suddenly as a ghost and Conn froze, thinking for one insane instant that she'd sensed him there, wanting her, had come out to—

No. Easing his breath out, he stepped even deeper into the shadows. She hadn't seen him. Didn't know he was out here. Had just gotten up to close the drapes against the moonlight and had paused to gaze out at the mountains.

Naked. God, she was naked.

Swallowing, Conn tried to tear his gaze from her, knowing it wasn't right to watch her like this. Hating himself when he couldn't look away, couldn't do anything but stand there, unseen, drinking in the sight of her like a dying man.

She stood there, one knee bent slightly, her left arm still raised. Her breasts were full and taut, the dark nipples taunting him with a flood of erotic memories from twelve years ago. Moonlight spilled down her shoulder and flank, along the curve of one hip and thigh, leaving tantalizing shadows in its wake that made his mouth go dry.

Another flood of memories assailed him. Textures. The heated silk of her, the erotic, musky scent of sex, the taste of her. Sounds…the rapid whisper of her breath against his throat as he loved her, the sound of his own breathing, fast and deep, the tiny, breath-caught moans, the way she'd finally just let go of her self-consciousness and had reached toward him with her body, moving with desperate urgency, legs tangling around his, urging him deeper, faster, harder….

And then, suddenly, she moved. She reached up languidly and, before he could even groan a denial, had pulled the draperies closed.

Andie was humming to herself when she walked into the dining room the next morning. With only about fifteen people needing service, the lodge staff had closed off most of the room, using only the far end where a wall of windows overlooked a breathtaking panorama of lake and mountains and cloud-tousled sky. The morning sun was pouring in, making the pine floors and walls glow like butter, and a refreshing breeze was meandering through a couple of open windows, carrying the scent of pine.

Some of Beck's people were seated at a round table by the nearest window and they glanced up at her, obviously torn between asking her to sit down out of politeness, and not wanting the competition in on their conversation. Smiling, she simply lifted her hand and called out a cheerful greeting, then gazed around as though looking for someone.

To her relief, Conn was there, sitting by himself at a spacious table, half-hidden from the others by an exuberant clump of tropical greenery. She walked over, smiling. "Hi. Want some company?"

He looked up and Andie stared at him in astonishment. "What on earth happened to you? You look like hell!"

"Didn't get much sleep last night," he growled.

"Really? I slept like a log." She sat down in the chair on the other side of the table. "I told you all that coffee was a bad idea. If we work late tonight, I'll make you some herbal tea."

"Perfumed dishwater," he muttered ungraciously, fastening his slightly bleary eyes on her. "How come you're so damn full of energy this morning?"

She shrugged, catching the eye of the waiter hovering discreetly behind the palms. "All this mountain air, probably. Marc and I walked up to Wolf Ridge this morning, and—"

"Walked?" His eye narrowed. "You and Marc? Walked?"

Andie looked at Conn. "Yes, Connor. Walked. It's quite simple—you just put one foot down in front of the other and pretty soon you're doing it. And frankly, you look as though you could use a good, stiff walk yourself this morning."

"A good, stiff drink maybe."

Andie eyed him carefully. "Are you hung over?"

"From twenty cups of coffee?"

"I just thought you might have spent part of last night toasting Judith goodbye again."

He managed a rough smile. "Trust me, one hangover per ex-wife is my limit."

The waiter appeared from seemingly nowhere, handing Andie a menu, filling her coffee cup, fussing with the cutlery. She handed the menu back without even opening it. "I'll just have coffee, orange juice and an English muffin, thanks."

"That's not going to keep you going all morning," Conn said as the waiter vanished as silently as he'd appeared.

Andie paused very slightly. There was no reason for her not to tell him. Except that every time she mentioned Marc

Beck's name, Conn got weird. "I...umm...had breakfast with Marc this morning."

Conn had lifted his glass of orange juice and was looking
at her over the rim. "Breakfast." He took a swallow of
juice. "In his room."

He said it blandly enough, but Andie heard the tightness
in his voice. "In his suite," she replied calmly, pouring
cream into her coffee and stirring it. "Do you have a problem with that?"

"I don't have a problem with that."

"You don't."

"Nope. Why should I?" He took another long swallow
of juice. "I can see where André what's his name might, but
not me."

"Alain," she said testily. "His name is Alain!" The
waiter appeared just then. He set a tall, frosted glass of orange juice in front of her; then, with a subdued flourish,
added a royal blue-and-gold china plate with two perfectly
toasted English muffins on it, followed by two small silver
serving dishes, one with whipped butter, the other with a
thick marmalade the color of melted gold. He fussed with
the centerpiece of daisies and sweet william for a moment,
then left.

"Did you and Marc have a good walk?"

There it was again! The question itself was innocent
enough, but there was something not-so-innocent under the
words, and it made Andie's eyes narrow. "What *is* your
problem, Connor?"

"Me?" He shrugged, looking as though he hadn't a clue
what she was talking about. "I don't have a problem."

"Like hell you don't," Andie said with precision.
"You've been on his case ever since you met him."

"He's just a little too slick for my liking, that's all."

"You think he's going to make trouble during negotiations with his father?" She thought about it, wondering
what Conn saw that she hadn't. He hadn't gotten this far on
good looks and charm alone; Conn Devlin had a mind for

business like a bear trap, and an instinct about people to match.

"He's just along for the ride," Conn said dismissively. "Desmond holds all the cards—and power—at Becktron."

Andie didn't say anything, simply looking at him, waiting.

"I don't like the way he looks at you," Conn growled after a moment. "I don't like the way he's always touching you. And I sure as *hell* don't like the way he was all over you yesterday at the helipad."

"Excuse me?" Andie gave a burst of laughter. "All over me? He shook my hand and gave me a peck on the cheek, and—"

"Mouth," Conn said shortly. "He kissed you on the mouth. And it sure as hell was no *peck*. I know a peck when I see it. That was no peck."

Andie rolled her eyes. "Give me a break! All right, so he kissed me. On the mouth. I admit it. Bring on the firing squad!"

Conn's eyes glittered slightly. "You like him, don't you?"

"More than I like you, right at this moment," Andie told him irritably. "You're doing it again, Connor. I told you not to do this anymore."

"Do what?"

"Meddle." She said the word loudly enough to make a couple of Beck's people look around in surprise. Biting back her impatience, she picked up a piece of muffin and slathered it with marmalade. "I don't meddle in your love life, Connor."

"Does the name Olivia Woodruff ring a bell?" he asked pleasantly enough.

"I wasn't meddling, I was giving you my opinion. *You* meddle."

"When have I ever meddled?" He sounded almost indignant. "Sure, I've given you advice now and again when I see you making a mistake. And maybe I've made a suggestion or two, but—"

Andie put the knife down with a bang. "A suggestion or two? I haven't dated a man in my entire life that you've approved of. They're too young, too old, too rich, not rich enough, they work too much, they're worthless layabouts. My God, you even had one of them *investigated!*"

"The man was wanted for tax evasion and fraud," Conn said between gritted teeth. "And what about that other loser you dated a few years ago? If I hadn't done a background check on the guy, you'd never have discovered he had a wife and two kids in Arizona until it was too late." His eyes narrowed suspiciously. "It *wasn't* too late, was it?"

"I was twenty-seven years old, for God's sake!"

"You mean it *was* too late?" His shoulders seemed to swell.

"No," Andie said tightly, "it was not too late. The fact you kept me working until midnight every single night he was in town had something to do with that, of course."

Conn looked pleased with himself. "See? I wasn't meddling, I was just looking out for you."

"You were meddling," Andie said darkly. "Alain happened to mention that someone's been asking around about him, too. There's even evidence that someone's running a financial check on him. But you wouldn't know anything about that, would you?"

She watched him struggle with it, torn between lying to her and putting himself in the line of fire. Finally he just shrugged and took a swallow of coffee, avoiding her eyes. "You can't be too careful about people these days."

"You stink."

It made him laugh. "Hey, what are good friends for?"

Andie swore she wasn't going to laugh. That she wasn't going to let him get away with this sort of behavior any longer. But in spite of her best intentions, she wound up grinning. "I don't know why I put up with you, Devlin."

He kissed the end of his finger, then reached across and planted it on her mouth. "Because you love me, darlin'. Why else?"

"You hope." She turned her head away as though angry and she concentrated on putting marmalade on another piece of muffin, not wanting him to see her eyes.

Someone stopped beside their table and she glanced up.

Marc Beck grinned down at her. "Hi, again."

Andie smiled. "Well, hi. Have a cup of coffee with us."

Marc glanced at Conn. "Well..."

"Oh, come on," Andie urged him, gesturing to the chair beside her. "Conn certainly doesn't mind. Do you, Connor?"

She smiled sweetly at him; Conn's eyes glittered.

"No. I don't mind at all. Please join us, Marc. I'd like that."

Andie gave Conn a look of warning, seeing something in his benign smile that she didn't like at all.

Marc grinned again and dropped into the chair. "Great idea, coming up here. We may get this deal with you hammered out yet, Devlin."

"One way or the other." Conn gave him a sleepy smile.

Marc glanced at Andie, obviously picking up some vibration of trouble ahead but uncertain of what was going on. "I, uh... My father says the two of you set up the first meeting this morning for about nine."

"If you can fit it in," Conn said agreeably. "Andie tells me you like to walk."

Mark nodded carefully. "Yeah, I like to get out and loosen up a bit. I run, actually. At home I put in about ten miles a day. How about you?"

Another pleasant smile. "I sail a bit. Play tennis. Squash."

"And killer handball," Andie put in. "Don't let him challenge you to a game—he plays for blood."

"Don't be a spoilsport, Andie," Conn said lazily. "Let him decide for himself. How about it, Beck? Up for a friendly little game?"

Andie saw Marc's eyes narrow slightly. "I think I'll pass, but thanks. Maybe some other time."

"Just say when." Conn took a swallow of coffee, leaning back in his chair and looking at Marc with deceptive friendliness. "So, tell me. Have you met Alain DeRocher yet?"

Andie's breath hissed and she stared at Conn disbelievingly.

Marc frowned, shaking his head. "No. No, I don't think I have. Is he with your company?"

"DeRocher?" Conn laughed. "Hell, no. He's Andie's fiancé."

"Fiancé?" Marc's head came up and he stared at her in surprise. "You're engaged, Andie? You never mentioned that."

"I am not engaged," Andie said through clenched teeth, giving Conn a look that should have melted steel plate but seemed to have no effect whatsoever on him. "Mr. Devlin is—as usual—quite mistaken."

"I thought you said Alain asked you to marry him," Conn said with just the right amount of apologetic surprise in his voice. "Hey, Andie, I'm sorry if I—"

"Look, I, uh, have some things to do before our meeting this morning. I think I'll pass on that coffee." Marc pushed his chair back, his face dark with anger. "I'll see you both later."

"Count on it," Conn said gently.

Andie watched Marc walk away, then turned on Conn furiously. "Of all the low-down, underhanded, rotten things to do!"

"What?" He gazed back at her, his expression of hurt innocence almost perfect.

"Don't *what* me, mister," she growled, pushing away from the table and standing up. "I don't know what you're playing at, but I want you to stop it—and I mean *now!* My life is none of your concern, Connor. So butt out, or I swear I will marry Alain and move to Quebec City and you can just find yourself another admin. *And* another best friend!"

Too far, Conn thought disconsolately as he watched Andie stalk across the dining room. He'd gone too far this time.

Swearing under his breath, he finished the rest of his coffee and shoved his chair back, getting to his feet. He was pushing Marc Beck too damn far, too, come to think of it. This deal wasn't in the bag yet, and if he couldn't control whatever was bugging him, he was going to blow it big-time.

He thought about it as he headed for the door. If he didn't know better, he'd swear it felt like *jealousy*. Except that didn't make any sense. Why would he be jealous of the men in Andie's life? He wanted her to be happy, didn't he?

Thinking about it just confused him even more. Divorce blues, that's what it was. He'd be back to normal in a week or two. Except if he didn't wise up, he was going to lose Andie before those couple of weeks were up.

Meetings. Three that day. They cleared up the question of pension benefits for those employees who would transfer from Becktron to Devlin Electronics. They settled on a severance package for those who wouldn't.

It was amazing what twelve people could accomplish with few distractions and a clear focus on the objective, Andie thought with satisfaction as she walked along the wide corridor to her suite. Another day or two like this and they'd have the Becktron sale in the bag and could all go home.

Although she was starting to like it up here. A lot. Smiling, she rubbed her damp hair with the towel. She'd just spent the hour with Margie, Bill Miller, Frank Czarnecki, Marc Beck and a couple of his people, going over the finer details of an addendum to the buy-out contract itself.

But not around a conference table. They'd all wound up—more by accident than design—in the giant hot tub that sat in its own cedar-and-pine gazebo in a grove of tall trees behind the lodge. It had been raining lightly but none of them had minded, relaxed and laughing and wreathed in pine-scented steam.

She didn't know where Conn was. He and Desmond Beck had spent most of the day and early evening sequestered in one of the luxury cabins down by the lake, working out heaven knew what. Which probably meant she'd be up half the night with Conn, going over tomorrow's strategy, depending on how things went.

Andie smiled again as she unlocked the door to her suite. Good thing he hadn't come along and found her in the hot tub with Marc Beck, or God knows what he'd have done this time. The thought had obviously occurred to Marc, too; he'd spent more time looking over his shoulder than working on the contract.

She locked the door behind her and wandered through the small kitchen, tossing her keys on the counter. Thinking about Marc Beck. He was interested, no doubt of that. And interesting.

Even more interesting was the fact she was thinking of him this way at all. If any man should be taking up her thoughts these days, it should be Alain DeRocher.

Sighing, Andie walked into the bedroom. Slipping out of the thick terry robe, she tossed it onto the bed and headed for the bathroom, already starting to peel herself out of the wet bathing suit.

Alain. She was going to have to make up her mind about that. Marrying him would fulfill her dreams: a warm and generous relationship with a man who cherished her, a home, children. Dreams she'd once hoped to share with Connor. The only thing that would be missing was the love.

And maybe, she found herself thinking dispassionately as she pulled open the glass door to the huge shower, she was just going to have to learn to live without that.

Tired. God, he was tired!

Conn rubbed the back of his neck and shrugged his shoulders, trying to work the knots free. He and Desmond had been at it all day, and he was worn-out and stiff.

He closed the door to his suite behind him and walked across to the small bar, pulling the fridge open. There were plenty of ice cubes. He tossed a handful into a glass and added a healthy shot of whiskey; then, carrying it in one hand and unbuttoning his shirt with the other, he headed for the bathroom.

Taking his drink right into the shower with him, he sipped it slowly while letting the hot water pound down on his back and shoulders, loosening taut muscles, working the tension free. Another few days of this and Devlin Electronics was going to be the big boy on the block, fulfilling every dream he'd ever had.

Or almost every dream. There were still one or two missing.

Idly, probing the memory as he might a sore tooth, he thought of Judith. And Liza. It had been years since he'd last spoken with her. They'd parted amicably enough, all considered, and had stayed in touch for a while. Then they'd both gotten busy with their respective lives and had drifted apart, she with her new husband and—last he'd heard—their three kids, him with Devlin Electronics.

Parting company with Judith had been less amicable. They'd each married the other with certain expectations in mind, and then had felt betrayed when those expectations hadn't been met. He'd wanted to kick back and enjoy life, raise a family, travel, have a little fun. Judith had had entirely different ideas.

He took another swallow of whiskey, wincing a little. Funny, how things worked out. He'd been on the cover of *Time* magazine twice, had been profiled in every major business magazine and paper in the country, had a net worth—even before the Becktron deal—of well into nine figures.

Yet, for all his financial success, his wizardry at not just recognizing the cutting edge of the industry but getting there first, he still couldn't seem to pick the right woman. Or make a marriage work.

Andie. Too bad he couldn't marry *her*. They got along great, she loved Devlin Electronics as much as he did, she knew him better than anyone, including his two ex-wives. Hell, they probably had a better chance than most people he knew to carve out a little happiness.

Then he smiled grimly and finished the whiskey in one long swallow. Until it fell apart, of course, and he lost his best friend in the world. And it would fall apart. It always did.

He shampooed his hair quickly, then turned off the water, toweled himself dry and pulled on a pair of ragged cutoffs and his old college sweatshirt. It was faded now and ripped a little here and there, but still wearable: a good-luck charm that had never let him down.

He had to grin suddenly, catching a glimpse of himself in the mirror. Hell, maybe that was the answer. Maybe instead of a tux, he should wear *it* to his next wedding.

Not that the thought of a *next* wedding was exactly a cheerful thought. In fact, the prospect of getting married again was about as pleasant as the prospect of having dental surgery.

He stuck his head through the connecting door into Andie's suite and called her name. There was no answer, and he frowned. It was after nine, damn it—where was she?

Unbidden, Marc Beck's grinning face flickered through his mind. His frown deepened and he pushed the door all the way open and walked in, instinctively looking around for any sign that Beck had been there.

Or was still there, Conn thought grimly, glancing at the half-open bedroom door.

He shook off the thought before it was even fully formed, telling himself he was losing it. Beck wasn't Andie's type, for one thing. And she'd never get involved with him while he and Beck's father were in the middle of negotiations.

And afterward? Hell, afterward, she had that damned Frenchman to deal with.

That thought made him frown even more as he walked across to the kitchen counter where they'd set up the fax machine and started looking through the incoming messages. All of a sudden she had men coming at her from every direction.

Sure, she'd always had a boyfriend or two hovering in the background—and why not, she was gorgeous. Although *that* hadn't really registered until just lately, either. But she'd never seemed to get very serious about any of them.

But now there was this DeRocher guy talking marriage and Andie talking weddings and kids and it was just getting out of hand, damn it.

Idly, he thought of calling DeRocher and telling him to back off. But odds were pretty good that Andie would find out—she always seemed to find out—and there would be some serious hell to pay.

So the best thing was probably just to stay out of it and wait for it to run its course. She didn't love the guy—that was pretty obvious. So Conn would just wait for her to realize that and unload DeRocher. Things would be back the way they should be—just the two of them against the world—and he could quit worrying.

It made him laugh out loud as he looked through the papers on the counter for the report Frank Czarnecki had put together on the estimated worth of Becktron's patents. That's how he felt some days—he and Andie against the world.

The report wasn't there and he glanced around the living room for Andie's briefcase. Frowning, he walked across and knocked on the bedroom door. Still no answer, although he could hear the shower running. He could see her briefcase, lying open on the bed surrounded by piles of loose paper, and he walked across to it.

He smiled a little as he caught a waft of her perfume on the air, hints of sandalwood and exotic oils and some underlying fragrance that always made him think of long hot nights, rumpled sheets and sex. It was subtle and faint, but effective as hell. And she didn't wear it half often enough, in his estimation.

Probably just as well, he decided as he started leafing through the pile of scattered papers on the bed. It would be mighty distracting to have her smelling that good *all* the time.

He didn't find the report, but he *did* find something else that intrigued him even more. A nightie. A pale apricot thing sheer enough to make him swallow hard, and he picked it up, running the cobwebby fabric though his fingers.

It disconcerted him, although he couldn't quite figure out why. Probably because he'd never given much thought to what Andie wore to bed. Had never given much thought to her *in* bed...except lately. Lately he seemed to be thinking about it a lot.

And this nightie? He frowned, holding it up to get a better look at it. This wasn't the kind of thing a woman wore to bed when she was alone, planning to do nothing more exciting than read a book or watch a late-night talk show. For that matter, it didn't look like the kind of thing Andie would buy for herself. Unless—

DeRocher. Question was, had he bought it for Andie in anticipation, or had she bought it herself for the same reason?

A better question might be, why did he think it was any of his business?

Swearing at himself, Conn tucked the nightie back under the scattered papers and hauled his mind back to the problem of the Becktron patents. He found Czarnecki's report just as the shower went off and he glanced at the half-open bathroom door a little guiltily. He could see the big mirror above the vanity and in it, Andie's reflection as she stepped out of the shower, wet and very naked.

Her reflection was nothing but a blur of tanned curves on the steamy mirror, but he swore and wrenched his gaze away and walked back into the living room, thinking that the

quicker they all got back to the city, the better it was going
to be for everyone concerned.

Rubbing her wet hair with a towel, Andie was still thinking about Alain as she walked out of the bedroom and down
the short corridor to the living room and kitchen. It took her
a moment to even realize Conn was there, sprawled across
the overstuffed sofa in front of the fireplace as though he
belonged there, frowning over a handful of papers.

He looked up, brows tugged together. "Is Czarnecki sure
about these figures?"

Clad only in her terry robe and a layer of body oil, Andie
hesitated, then walked through to the kitchen area. "Come
on in, Connor. Make yourself at home. Tea?"

He looked at her for a blank moment, then winced.
"Sorry. I did knock, but you didn't hear me. And yeah,
tea's fine—but only if it's the real stuff and not those weeds
and berries you're always brewing up."

"Real stuff." She smiled slightly and popped a couple of
bags of an herbal blend into the china teapot she'd found in
one of the cupboards. "Frank's sure about those figures. If
anything, they're on the conservative side."

Conn looked back down at the sheet of paper he was
holding and gave a low whistle.

"How did your meeting with Desmond go today?"

"Good." A slow smile tipped his strong mouth up on one
side. "Better than good. What about you?"

"I spent most of the day going over their inventory. Talk
about a nightmare!"

"Can you get a handle on it?"

"I'll get a handle on it."

Conn's grin widened. "You're not really going to marry
old DeRocher and leave all this, are you?"

The kettle whistled and Andie turned the heat off, then
poured boiling water into the teapot. "So make me an offer I can't refuse," she said lightly. "I haven't said yes to
Alain *yet*." Smiling mischievously, she set the pot of tea,
two cups and spoons and a bowl of honey on a tray and

carried them across to the sofa. "Maybe I'll marry Marc Beck instead. He seems quite interested."

"Too damned interested," Conn growled as she set the tray on the end table beside him. "What's all this talk lately about getting married, anyway?"

"You're the one who brought it up."

"So then I'm the one who's telling you to forget it. Marriage isn't all it's cracked up to be." Conn reached across and tossed the papers he was holding onto the floor. "In fact, it isn't *anything* it's cracked up to be."

"Conn..." Andie sat down on the edge of the sofa beside him, reaching down to smooth a tangle of dark hair off his forehead. "Don't be too hard on yourself over this. You made a couple of bad choices, that's all. The next time will probably be everything you've ever dreamed it would be."

"The next time?" He smiled dryly, then slipped both arms loosely around her waist and pulled her down across his chest. "Darlin', who the hell says there's going to be a next time?"

Six

Andie went still with surprise, hardly daring to breathe. Conn cradled her against him as though it was the most natural thing in the world to do, his breath stirring her hair slightly, arms folded around her comfortably. And then, after a moment or two, she realized he probably wasn't even aware of what he was doing.

She was his best friend and he needed the touch of another person, so what more normal thing to do than reach for her?

Telling herself it couldn't hurt, she relaxed against his broad chest, breathing in the warm, familiar scent of him, feeling his body heat soak through the terry robe right to her soul. His heartbeat was solid and slow and regular beneath her and she closed her eyes, knowing it wasn't right to even pretend for these few minutes that he really cared. That this casual embrace was anything more than a need for comfort, and she was there for any reason other than mere convenience.

"You know what I was thinking?" he said after a minute or two, his voice just a rumble.

"I'm afraid to ask." He was rubbing her back absently, and Andie slipped her arm around him.

"I was thinking that when this Becktron deal is finished, we should take a week off and sail up the coast. Remember when we were in college and always talked about doing that? We never did make it."

"You were practically *married* to Billy Soames," she reminded him. "You guys spent every minute together, working on your computer design. Then there was Charlotte, and Anne, and Veronica, and—"

"Okay, okay," he said with a chuckle, "I get the point. But you didn't have a lot of time, either, with all those guys hanging around you. I remember Adam—he always looked like he'd just stepped out of *The Great Gatsby*. And Rod, the biker. And—"

"Rod was *not* a biker," she protested, laughing. "That old Triumph he rode was a family heirloom, practically."

"Uh-huh. There was that other guy, the athletic major with more muscles than brains who tried to kill me that night in Dooby's Pub."

"Richard Reece, and you started it by telling—who was that girl you were with that night, the one with the *huge* breasts?"

"Ashleigh," he said dryly. "And contrary to your opinion on the matter, they *were* real."

"I'm sure," she replied just as dryly. "And I don't blame Richard for getting mad. You kept telling Ashleigh that there was a direct link between pumping iron and brain damage."

"He had an equally high opinion of engineering students. What did he call Billy? A pencil-necked geek."

"Billy *was* a pencil-necked geek," Andie reminded him gently. "He was sweet and nice, but let's face it—he'd wear the same shirt for weeks on end, his hair always looked like it had been chewed by rats and he lived on pizza and soft drinks, to the detriment of both complexion and breath. I always liked Billy a lot, but he was in another world half the time.''

''Well, that pencil-necked geek's been married to the same woman for ten years and has four kids, so I guess he had something going for him besides an IQ that's off the scale.''

''He married that tiny little chemistry major, didn't he? Corinne. She absolutely adored him even back then.''

''I was thinking about Billy today. He'd go nuts if he could see some of the work Beck's research people are into. They branched out into virtual reality and artificial intelligence even before we did at Devlin, and I have to tell you, they're light-years ahead of us in some areas. Beck figured to use it in the stuff he was doing for the navy, but when the military contracts dropped off a couple of years ago, everything kind of stopped. But what they *do* have, wow....''

Andie had to smile, hearing the old excitement in his voice. ''What's Billy doing now?''

''Last I heard, he'd sold his software company and was working as a consultant. Wish I could convince him to come on board with us. I could sure use some of that genius he has with computers.''

''So ask him.''

There was a long and thoughtful silence. ''Do you think he would?''

''Sometimes all you have to do is ask, Conn.''

''It'd be like old times.'' He tightened his arms around Andie and kissed the top of her head. ''Billy and Corinne, you and me. Hell, we'd be invincible.''

You and me. Andie smiled against Conn's chest, refusing to allow herself to even think it could ever happen. ''Not if it means you're going to start beating up all my boyfriends again.''

''I just beat up one. Fred Something. And he deserved it, groping you like that. You were thirteen years old!''

"I'd forgotten about Fred. I was thinking about Ricky Hapgood, in fifth grade. And James Munro in sixth grade. And—"

"I caught Hapgood trying to kiss you behind the school buses, and Munro used to drop beetles down your back."

"And Eddie Cantrelli in seventh grade, and—"

"I didn't like the way he always had his arm around you."

"And Chad Matthews in my first year of college."

"Ditto. The guy was a surf bum, all muscle and brawn."

"He was cute."

"He had the IQ of a piece of celery."

"Unlike the women you used to date in college, of course, who were all Rhodes scholars masquerading as pinup girls."

Conn had to grin. "Yeah, yeah, okay. But for the record, I *did* date some pretty bright women, too. Hell, I dated you for a couple of months, and you're so bright, you scare me."

"Until you threw me over for Liza."

Conn was quiet for a moment, thinking back to those days. He'd believed in magic back then, had believed in dreams. "Not one of my smarter decisions," he said thoughtfully, kissing the top of Andie's head again. "I should have gone after you that summer. I never felt right about the way things ended between us after that weekend up at Mount Baker. Maybe if I hadn't been so caught up in that damned computer Billy and I were designing, or if you'd stayed in Seattle instead of taking that summer job down in California... hell, who knows."

He rested his chin on the top of her head and stared into the fire, thinking idly that they might have been good together if they'd given it a chance. But he'd waited too long, and anything she'd felt for him had changed and he'd missed his chance.

"I guess you just don't know what you've got until you've lost it," he muttered half to himself.

Andie didn't say anything. She was nestled against him as though she belonged there, comfortable, natural, fitting into the contours of his body as though somehow designed for him.

Funny, how he'd never really noticed that before. He noticed it now, though—perhaps a little too vividly, very aware of the pressure of her breasts against his chest, the curve of hip and bottom against his lower belly, thigh against thigh. And he could feel the warmth of her, too, carrying with it the scent of shower gel and soap and clean feminine skin.

He thought of holding her the other morning, of the feel of her skin, the taste of her mouth . . . thoughts that led to other thoughts. . . .

He had to get out of here.

Now.

Teeth gritted, he pushed Andie gently away from him and sat up. "Gotta go, darlin'," he murmured, not meeting her gaze in case she could read even some of what he thinking in his eyes. Because if she did, she'd kill him. Right here, right now.

She didn't say anything. Just nodded, her head down slightly so her hair partially obscured her features. Her robe had come loose so the front gaped a little, and he let his eyes follow the neckline down, tracing the delicate curve of her throat, the soft swell of the top of her breast, her skin smooth and lightly sheened with body oil. . . .

Taking a deep breath, Conn leaned over and gathered up the papers he'd tossed aside earlier, trying to get his rambling thoughts back under control. What the *hell* was happening to him, anyway? It was as though he'd never seen her before or something.

This was *Andie,* for crying out loud! *His* Andie. Hell, he'd always known she was gorgeous. A man would have to be blind *not* to notice.

But that had never been an issue. He hadn't coaxed her to work for him because she was beautiful, or because watching her walk across a room was a pleasure in itself, or because she had legs that would make a grown man weep.

There were plenty of women around who fit that bill if all he'd wanted was looks.

He'd wanted her at Devlin Electronics because she was his friend, and he respected and trusted her. Because she had a mind that could cut braised steel. Because she could juggle eighteen crises at a time and never lose her cool. Because she laughed at his jokes. Because she made *him* laugh. Because when he was around her he felt like a kid again, as though nothing was impossible and every dream he ever had could come true.

Taking another deep breath, he got to his feet. He needed a woman. The last eighteen or so months without sex had messed up his mind, no two ways about it. While he was still married to Judith he'd just put his libido on hold, but now...man, now he was even ready to hit on his best friend!

Olivia, he found himself thinking a little desperately. Maybe when they got back to Seattle he'd call Liv.

Andie was looking at him, a little frown between those lovely brows, her eyes searching his, almost as though she wanted to say something but didn't know how.

And he had a pretty good idea what it was. If he wasn't careful, he wasn't just going to have to find himself a new assistant, but a new best friend as well. "Let's call it a night," he said quietly. "Beck isn't going anywhere. We can go over this report of Czarnecki's in the morning."

Andie nodded, shoving her hands into the deep pockets of her robe. She was tempted to ask him to stay, but it was hard being this close to him. In Seattle, in the office, she had her professional persona as a barrier between her and her feelings. But here...the moonlight, the solitude, the fire. All conspired to make her wish things that could never be, to taunt herself with possibilities.

She strolled beside him as he walked toward the connecting door to his suite. "You never did drink your tea."

"Rain check." He grinned down at her, then leaned one broad shoulder against the door frame as though deliberately postponing going through. "You know," he said very carefully, his gaze holding hers with only a hint of mischief. "We, uh, *could* ... Well, for old times' sake, we could—"

"Are you hitting on me, Connor Devlin?" she asked with a laugh, leaning on the wall beside him and gazing up into his grey-green eyes.

"Well..." His grin widened. "Yeah."

Andie laughed again, tempted, for one fleeting moment, to say yes just to see his expression. Instead, she just reached up and took a fistful of sweatshirt fabric and pulled him toward her. "Kiss me, you mad fool, and then go have a cold shower and go to bed."

"My pleasure, ma'am..." He slipped one warm hand around the back of her neck, cradling her head, and brought his mouth down over hers more fully than she'd expected.

It was supposed to have been just a casual good-night kiss, but Conn found himself kissing her slowly and deeply, taking his time over it, letting himself enjoy every wondrous moment of it.

She gave a muffled squeak after a moment or two and drew her mouth from his, fingers still tangled up in the front of his sweatshirt, her eyes wide and a little unfocused. "Wh-what was *that* all about?" She sounded breathless.

"Damned if I know," he admitted with a chuckle. Her hair was like silk between his fingers and he ran his thumb up the side of her throat, loving the softness of her skin. "But we could always do it again and see what happens."

"No." Taking a deep breath, she stepped back, shaking her head. "No, I don't think that would be a good idea."

Conn had the sudden thought that if he really wanted to— *really* wanted to—he could probably talk her into bed. He found himself looking down at her, actually tempted to try it. It would be nice having her warmth tucked into the emptiness of his bed, to turn to her in the night and make love to her....

Except he'd have to face her in the morning and try to explain just what the hell he thought he'd been doing. And facing her wouldn't even be as bad as having to face himself with the same question. It would change everything between them, change everything they were to each other, and he wasn't ready to lose her, too.

"No, you're probably right," he said quietly, leaning down to kiss her again, but lightly this time. "We've got a good thing going here, right? It would be a shame to spoil it with something as self-indulgent and shallow as a night of spectacular sex." He gazed down at her as he said it, half hoping she'd say, "Here's to self-indulgence and shallowness," and "Let's go to bed, cowboy—we'll figure something out in the morning."

And he thought for half an instant that she was going to do just that. She stood there, looking up at him with her lips half-parted, gaze searching his intently. It was one of those breath-held moments that seems to go on forever, and Conn actually started to reach for her just as she stepped back, laughing very softly, her eyes glowing with mischief.

"Yes, I suppose it would. Best friends are hard to come by—isn't that what we agreed?"

Grinning broadly, Conn reached out to comb a handful of silken dark hair off her forehead with his fingers. "Of course, we *could* have been wrong...."

Her smile turned thoughtful and she shook her head, looking a bit wistful. "No, I don't think we were. Not that I don't think a night of sex with you wouldn't *be* spectacular, mind you."

In spite of himself, Conn had to give a bark of laughter. "I don't know about that, darlin'—I'm so out of practice I might wind up just embarrassing myself."

"Somehow I doubt that," Andie murmured, soft lips curving up in a sly smile. She put her fingers against his chest and pushed him gently backward through the door. "Good night, Connor. Sweet dreams."

"If you get restless in the night, you know where to find me." Still grinning, he gave her an outrageous wink, then closed the door gently behind him—more for her sake than his—and headed for bed. Although he couldn't see himself getting any sleep for a long, long while....

But to Conn's surprise, he did get a half-decent night's sleep, although his dreams had been pretty wild.

And X-rated, he found himself thinking with a grin as he adjusted the brightness on the screen of his laptop computer. If Andie had any *idea* of the things the two of them had been up to in his dreams last night, she'd staple his hide to his office wall. Or use that sterling silver letter opener on her desk to divest him of one or two more critical bits of his anatomy.

He shrugged his shoulders to ease the tension across them and leaned back in the chair as his computer loaded in the new program he'd called up, still grinning. He was on his own this morning. Beck had called early to say he and a couple of his top honchos were heading back to Seattle to work out some final details, and wouldn't be back until late.

Which meant they were in the home stretch, Conn thought with satisfaction. He'd be glad when it was finally over. This had never been his favorite part. The endless meetings and strategy, the deal-making, the dickering—all wore his patience thin after a while. He wanted to *make* things, not talk about them. All the boardroom mind games in the world couldn't match the visceral excitement of watching one of his engineers put the finishing touches on a prototype, then turning it on and having it work—really *work*—for the first time.

Andie, thank heaven, seemed to understand that. Over the past nine years she had taken on more and more of the actual day-to-day details of running Devlin Electronics, leaving him free to work with design and engineering.

If he lost her...

He narrowed his eyes slightly. Maybe he would make a phone call to DeRocher this afternoon. Just a friendly little suggestion to back off. Andie would kill him if she ever found out, of course, but it would be worth the risk. She didn't love DeRocher. She couldn't love him. He wasn't right for her at all. Too old, too stodgy, too...hell, too everything!

And Marc Beck? Not him, either.

Problem was, Andie was just too damn good for most of the men she met. She needed someone who knew how special she was. Someone who could make her laugh with just a look, and knew that her favorite flowers were snapdragons and that her favorite movie was *Casablanca*. Someone who could rub her back the right way, and make her a margarita just how she liked it, and was willing to spend hours rooting around in musty old bookstores looking for those volumes of romantic poetry she loved.

Somebody like *him*, Conn thought irritably.

Maybe marrying your best friend wasn't such a bad idea after all. If nothing else, at least you could count on sharing a good laugh now and again.

Except he'd never convince her of that. As far as Andie was concerned, friendship and romance did not mix.

Which was just as well, because he didn't have a damned thing to offer her anyway. Two failed marriages wasn't exactly the kind of thing that inspired confidence. With his record, even Andie—who knew him better than anybody— would be a fool to take a chance on him.

Hell.

He rubbed the back of his neck and glowered at the computer screen, not making much sense of it. Not really interested in making any sense of it. He'd been listening to the faint sound of voices and splashing and laughter for a while now without really registering what it was. But now, suddenly, he found himself wishing he was out there with whoever was in the pool rather than in here, working. Or pretending to work.

Restless, he got up and walked across to the window. There were four of them in the water: Margie, Frank Czarnecki, one of Bill Miller's people and Andie. They were playing some game with a beach ball, which seemed to consist mainly of trying to drown each other, and he grinned, amused at the sight of Frank Czarnecki in bathing trunks and not a computer in sight.

Someone rapped on the door of his suite and he shouted at whoever it was to come in, smiling as Andie shot up out of the water to grab the ball. She took off for the far end of the pool with it, everyone else in hot pursuit.

"I have those financial records you wanted."

Conn glanced around as Marc Beck walked into the room. "I thought you'd gone into Seattle with your father."

Mark shook his head, tossing a handful of papers down on the table where Conn had been working. "Nope. He and his bean counters have things under control. I'd just be in the way."

Conn leaned one shoulder against the wall and looked at Marc curiously. "You know, I haven't been able to help notice that you don't seem very concerned that your father's selling Becktron out from under you. You *are* his only son. It seems to me that—"

"—that I'd be chomping at the bit to take over?" Marc grinned easily, coming across to look out the window. "Hell, no. Becktron was always my dad's baby, not mine. Frankly, I'm just as glad to see it go. Our bread and butter were the big military contracts, and when they went the way of the cold war, our days were numbered. We have the choice of retooling and trying to start over again, or bowing out gracefully." Marc gazed down at the pool thoughtfully.

Andie was out of the water now, stretched out in a deck chair in a peacock blue bathing suit that left a hell of a lot more firm, tanned flesh exposed than Conn thought absolutely necessary. He'd forgotten just how good she looked in a bathing suit. And Beck, obviously, had noticed it, too.

"Are you, um..." Beck looked at him speculatively. "This isn't any of my business, but you and Andie seem pretty tight."

"We are," Conn said abruptly.

"She says you used to live beside each other when you were kids. That you grew up together."

"That's right." What the hell had they been doing, trading life histories?

"She says you went to college together, too. That you've always been sort of best friends."

"Not sort of," Conn said testily. "We *are* best friends." He gave Beck a mildly hostile look. "Are you going anywhere with this, or just fishing?"

Marc just looked at him calmly. "She seems to think a hell of a lot of you. I just wanted to know if there's anything more to it than that."

The question, Beck's sly way of getting at it, irritated Conn unreasonably. "Why don't you ask Andie?"

"I did." Another speculative look. "She said you're not romantically involved. But..." Beck smiled very faintly, his eyes holding Conn's. "I figured you might have other ideas."

"Such as?" Conn kept his voice deliberately soft.

Marc laughed quietly, bracing one shoulder against the window frame casually. "She's a hell of a woman, Devlin. To be honest, I can't figure out why you haven't already snapped her up. She's just about everything a man could want in a woman."

"I told you," Conn growled, looking down at the pool. At Andie. "We're just good friends."

"So you don't mind if I...?" He left it delicately hanging.

"If you *what?*"

"No more games, Devlin," Marc said with a lazy smile. "I like Andie. I like her a lot. And I'm interested in pursuing it further. I just want to make sure you're okay with that."

"It's got nothing to do with me," Conn said mildly. "You should be having this conversation with Alain DeRocher, in Quebec City."

"Andie and I have talked about DeRocher. I don't think it's particularly serious. Not from Andie's side, anyway."

Conn looked at Beck. Had Andie told him that? Hell, she wouldn't even discuss DeRocher with *him!*

"You don't have to worry about this interfering in your negotiations with Becktron." Marc smiled again and shrugged away from the wall. "I'll stay at a discreet distance until the deal is finished. As you pointed out the other day, until this deal goes through, you and I are still competitors."

Marc left then, strolling across the room and out the door as casually as he'd come in, leaving Conn gazing down at the pool. Andie was talking with Margie now, laughing in the sun, completely unaware that he was watching her. That he and Beck had been planning her future.

Beck, anyway. Conn smiled. Beck had a hell of a surprise coming if he thought it was going to be that easy. He'd come in here talking as though it was already a done deal, as though the decision was his and that Andie would just naturally fall into his arms.

Conn knew her better than that.

Or did he? Conn narrowed his eyes slightly as he looked down at her. He'd always *thought* he knew Andie Spencer better than he knew anyone. And yet, in the past few days, she'd hit him with a couple of surprises, the fact she was actually contemplating marrying DeRocher being just one of them.

He thought of Beck. Thought of Beck with Andie.

You and I are still competitors....

Damn straight. Grinning, he turned away from the window, reaching down to shut off the computer as he walked by the table. And may the best man win, sport. May the best man win.

Frank Czarnecki was a new man.

Andie started rubbing her wet hair with the towel just to hide her grin. She had no idea what it was—the mountain

air, the vacation atmosphere, the fact that Margie looked
good in a bathing suit—but *something* had turned Frank
into a pretty fair imitation of a suave guy. He was talking.
He was laughing. He was relaxed and having fun. He was
even flirting.

Still grinning, Andie leaned back and watched the two of
them. Margie was glowing like a sixteen-year-old in love for
the first time, eyes sparkling, cheeks pink. They were sitting on a big towel beside the pool, knees almost touching,
leaning toward each other in that way a man and woman did
when the rest of the world had ceased to exist and there's
just the two of them.

A tiny flicker of envy shot through her, watching them
laughing like that. Those first few days of falling in love
were unlike anything else in the world—every heartbeat im-
bued with magic, each moment a new discovery, each breath
drawn filled with joy. The world became a wondrous place
where every word and glance and touch held meaning and
tenderness.

It had been a long while since she'd felt that magic.

She let the towel fall into her lap and stared across the
pool at the mountains, a flood tide of sadness welling up
through her, making her eyes prickle. It was silly, feeling like
this. She had everything. Everything a woman could want.

Someone—someone decidedly and deliciously male—
suddenly sat on the chaise longue behind her and wrapped
two strong arms around her middle and nibbled the back of
her neck.

She smiled. "Good morning, Connor."

"How'd you know it was me?" he asked with a soft
laugh, rubbing his nose against her ear. "Could have been
Marc Beck."

"Marc Beck has better manners than to accost a woman
at nine in the morning."

Conn's arms tightened slightly and he kissed the side of
her throat. "That's the only way you knew? My timing?"

"And your after-shave." She grinned. "And this." She ran her fingertip along the white scar meandering along his forearm. "You nearly died in that car accident."

" 'Only the good die young.' Isn't that what you told me when you came to see me in the hospital?" He nuzzled the nape of her neck. "I'd just turned seventeen, was half-drunk on beer and cheap wine, and our team had just beat the hell out of the competition. You made me swear an oath that night, remember?"

"I remember." It still made her go cold, just thinking about walking into that hospital room and seeing him lying there surrounded by tubes and wires.

"You made me swear I'd never drink and drive again. That if I did, our friendship was over." He let his lips rest on her throat for a moment. "You scared the hell out of me that night, Andie. I remember looking into your eyes and realizing you weren't kidding. That if I messed up, I'd never see you again."

"It worked, didn't it?" she teased gently.

"Damn right." He sounded almost subdued. "I haven't broken that promise in sixteen years."

"Well, don't get any ideas about breaking it now. That promise still holds."

"Not a chance." He was silent for a long moment. "I don't want to lose you, Andie," he finally said very quietly. "You mean more to me than just about anything."

Andie frowned slightly, turning in his loosened embrace so she could look at him. He looked pensive and thoughtful, his eyes holding none of the teasing she'd expected. "Connor, what are you talking about? What's going on that I should know about?"

"I was going to ask you the same question."

"Meaning?"

"Beck."

"The elder or the younger?"

Conn didn't smile.

Andie sighed. "Conn, I don't know what's gotten into you lately. You never used to get all bent out of shape about the men in my life. You always meddled and gave me advice I didn't need, but you never behaved like this. You're acting like a jealous husband."

"And you've never talked about getting married before, either," he said with more feeling than she suspected he'd intended. He frowned, looking annoyed. "Hell, I don't know why I'm acting like this, either. Maybe it's losing Judith, maybe... I don't know. It just seems as though you're the only thing I have in my life that I can count on, and now you're talking about marrying DeRocher and moving to Canada."

"I told you I haven't made up my mind yet," Andie said gently.

"Yeah, well, if it's not DeRocher, maybe it'll be Beck. And if not him, some other guy." He looked at her for a long, thoughtful while. "I guess I just never thought about you getting married, Andie. That was always something *I* did." He managed a flicker of a smile. "I guess I just never realized until recently that I will lose you one day. Sooner or later, it's going to happen. And I'm having trouble dealing with that."

"Well, you could always marry me yourself and keep it in the family." She had to laugh out loud at his expression, and she rocked forward and kissed him soundly on the mouth, astonished at how well she pretended it didn't matter. "Joke, Devlin. Just another little joke." He gave a grunt she couldn't quite decipher, eyeing her a little suspiciously, then nodded toward Frank and Margie, who were so engrossed with each other, they hadn't even noticed Conn. "What's going on with those two? Some problem with Becktron that no one's told me about?"

Andie looked at Conn in exasperation. "You know, Connor, sometimes it's as though you're in another world." She gave a snort. "*In* another world, nothing. *From* another world is more like it. You really don't have a clue sometimes, do you?''

''I don't have a clue what you're talking about,'' he muttered irritably. ''What the hell did I say?''

''Oh...forget it!'' Rolling her eyes in frustration, she shoved him off the chaise and got to her feet, snatching up her towel and wrapping it around her shoulders. ''I'm going for a walk.''

''With Marc Beck?''

''If I can find him, yes.''

''Forget it.'' He fell into step beside her and dropped his arm casually around her shoulders, tugging her against him as they walked into the lodge. ''We're going riding. Up to Wolf Lake. I've talked with the guy who rents the horses and it's all set up. And the chef's putting together a lunch to take with us.''

''Riding? Lunch?'' Andie stopped dead and turned to look up at him. ''Connor, that's nuts! It's supposed to rain, for one thing. In fact, the weather cast says it might snow tonight at higher altitudes. We can't just—''

''Why not?''

''I—'' She stopped. ''What do you mean, why not?''

''Just what I said. Desmond Beck won't be back until later tonight, and there's nothing urgent we need to work on. You used to love horseback riding.''

''Well, I...still do. I guess.'' She thought about it, the idea definitely intriguing. ''I haven't been on a horse in about a hundred years.''

''All the more reason to go.'' He grinned at her coaxingly. ''Come on, Andie. You're always telling me I work too hard. That I need to take off some time to just have fun. After the Becktron deal goes through, we're going to be up to our necks in work—who knows when we'll get another opportunity like this. I say we go for it while we have the chance.''

It was tempting. Very tempting. ''Only if you admit that this doesn't have anything to do with the fact we haven't spent a day together just having fun for years. Or that I think you work too hard. You're just trying to get me away from Marc Beck.''

His grin broadened. "Damn right."

"I *could* just invite him to come with us," she taunted.

"Too dangerous. The trail up to Wolf Lake is pretty narrow in places. I'd hate like hell to see him go over a cliff."

"You mentioned lunch."

"Four courses. Wine. Dessert." The grin widened wickedly. "Triple-Threat Chocolate Surprise."

"Triple bypass is more like it," Andie said with a laugh, knowing the battle was already half over. "You're bad news, Devlin. You always were."

"The worst." Laughing, he dropped his arm around her shoulders again and pulled her against him, tucking her comfortably into the curve of his body. "I grabbed your leather jacket out of the trunk of the car, but bring along a sweater."

"And if it rains?"

"We'll eat chocolate pudding."

Andie laughed again, wondering why she let him manipulate her so easily. "It'll lead to some speculation amongst the troops, having us disappear together for the day."

"So let's take Margie. She could use a day off. And it's not like we're secret lovers or something."

As she knew only too well, Andie thought. But she managed a smile. "I don't think Margie would appreciate being dragged up to Wolf Lake to play chaperon for the day. She's got other things on her mind. But," she added with a sly, sidelong glance at him, "I'll bet Marc would *love* to come with us."

Conn's retort—earthy and pungently Anglo-Saxon—was just two words long.

Seven

"So, was this a good idea, or what?" Conn grinned broadly. "Admit it, darlin'. This was a good idea."

Andie was ahead of him on the narrow, winding trail, riding a chestnut gelding whose glossy hide was just about the exact shade of red-brown as Andie's hair.

She tipped her head back and laughed, not even bothering to look around at him. "Yeah, Devlin, this was a good idea. As long as it doesn't rain."

"It's not going to rain." Although he winced a little as he said it, giving the sky a speculative glance. It didn't look promising, to be truthful about it. Dark clouds were piling up around the crests of the mountains to their right, and he could have sworn he'd heard a rumble of thunder a few minutes ago.

But he wasn't about to tell Andie that.

Family rumor had it that there was some Ogalala Sioux blood in Andie's background somewhere, and whenever he saw her on horseback, Conn was inclined to believe it. She

sat the chestnut as though born to ride, well balanced and
relaxed, keeping her weight in the stirrups and not the saddle, adjusting to the gelding's stride without even thinking
about it. It took no effort at all to see her flattened along the
back of a spotted pony, flying across open prairie with the
wind in her hair.

The vision made him grin and he lifted his face to the sun,
glad he'd come up with this last-minute scheme. Andie had
been right—the main idea *had* been to keep her away from
Marc Beck for the day—but there was no denying they'd
both benefit from a day off. It had been a hell of a long time
since he'd just kicked back and had some fun. Longer still
since he'd kicked back with Andie. And who knew how
much longer they'd have together?

The trail wound upward between Wolf and Fortress
mountains, following Wolf Creek as it twisted and snaked
its way through rock and dense forest. In some places, the
trail was wide and gently sloped, canopied by huge pine and
mountain hemlock and Pacific yew. In others, it was no
more than a narrow thread inching along the shoulder of
one mountain or the other, solid rock to one side and a sheer
drop to the other.

Wolf Creek fretted along beside them, as clear as glass
and bitterly cold, the bottle-green water rushing noisily
down the rock-strewn streambed. The mountains had closed
in and rose on all sides, their green-cloaked peaks scallop-
ing the sky, dotted here and there with outcroppings of rock
and patches of snow.

And then, suddenly, they were at the top.

Andie reined up so abruptly that the buckskin mare Conn
was riding nearly collided with the gelding. The mare gave
a snort and reared slightly, but Conn reined her in sharply
and brought her up beside Andie.

The mountains fell away to either side, opening up an al-
pine meadow so lush with wildflowers that the whole scene
looked like a Monet watercolor, just an exuberant explosion of blues and pinks, whites and yellows, violets...

every color of the rainbow. The air was filled with their perfume and Conn took a deep breath of it, grinning at the expression on Andie's face.

"Nice, huh?"

"It's incredible!" She looked around at him, her eyes sparkling with delight. "How did you know?"

Conn shrugged, feeling almost ridiculously pleased at her reaction. "One of the chambermaids was telling me about it. She and her boyfriend were up here yesterday. She said the timing's perfect—that in another week most of the color will be gone. So, I figured it was a real shame to waste it...."

"You know, you can really be a sweetheart when you want to be." Laughing, she reached across and slipped her hand into one of his. "This almost makes up for all those nasty cracks you've been making about Alain."

"If a bunch of flowers get you this mellowed out, I can hardly wait 'til we get to the Triple-Threat Chocolate Surprise."

There was a sudden low rumble from somewhere behind them and Andie looked around thoughtfully. "*That,* Tonto, was thunder. I thought you said we wouldn't get rain. Some weatherman you are."

"Is it raining?"

"Not yet, hotshot, but by the look of those clouds, it's going to be pouring before long."

Conn glanced at the sky. Even as he watched, dark clouds spilled over the crest of the mountain toward them, turbulent and bilious with rain. He swore under his breath, then pulled the mare's head out of a patch of clover and gave her a nudge with his heels. "Wolf Lake is about a mile ahead. And I'd say we'd be smart to quit talkin' and start ridin'."

Andie tightened the reins on the gelding, balancing herself easily in the saddle as he snorted and pranced half around, throwing his head impatiently. She looked doubtful. "It's not going to be any drier up there than back here. I hate to say this, but maybe we should head back."

"We've come too far—it's between us and the lodge. And I don't want to be caught by a bad thunderstorm on that ridge over Fortress Mountain. Even if we don't get nuked by lightning, that trail looks like it would wash out in a heavy rain."

He saw a flicker of concern on Andie's face and grinned. "Hey, trust me. I know this area like I know my own backyard, remember? Dad and I camped all over these mountains when I was a kid."

"The last time you said, 'Hey, trust me,' I wound up with my leg in a cast for seven weeks."

"So how was I supposed to know the wheel was going to come off the wagon when we went over that last bump?"

"And how did I ever let you talk me into riding down Suicide Hill in that crummy old wagon of yours in the first place?" Andie tugged the gelding around and kicked him gently in the ribs. "It's a miracle we didn't break our necks."

"But we almost made it, didn't we?" Conn reminded her with a wide grin. "It was a hell of a ride while it lasted."

"Until we hit the crest of that last hill and were airborne for about fifty feet. Until we crash-landed and the wheel fell off and we both did cartwheels the rest of the way down the hill." She grinned back. "But yeah, it was a hell of a ride while it lasted."

Andie's eyes locked with his and Conn was suddenly twelve years old again and having the time of his life. They'd had something special back then. Still had something pretty special: a friendship durable enough to survive over two decades' worth of ups and downs, bad decisions, good decisions, marriages, divorces, love affairs, successes and failures.

He felt something well up through him—a warm flood of emotions that caught him by surprise, intense and confusing in their complexity. He grinned at her again, then pulled the mare around and dug his heels into her ribs. "Come on, Cochise," he called to Andie as he galloped by her. "Let's ride!"

Andie gave a whoop and brought the gelding around, nudging him with her knees and loosening the reins. He gave a snort and half reared, then was streaking after the mare at a full gallop, ears back, long neck stretched out.

He caught up with the mare about halfway across the meadow and pulled ahead, with Andie laughing so hard, she was having trouble staying in the saddle, hair flying every which way, having no idea at all where she was going. The mare closed the gap and then she and the gelding were pounding down the long slope toward the end of the meadow at a flat-out gallop, ears back, hooves churning up bits of grass and dirt, muscles rippling with each long, powerful stride.

Conn shouted something as they neared the trees and Andie slowed the gelding, having to struggle to get him back under control. He slewed around, fighting the bit and rearing, throwing his head impatiently as she reined him in tightly. Conn pulled the mare up and the two horses jostled and nipped at each other, blowing hard and dancing around.

Conn was still laughing, his cheeks flushed with the wind, hair tousled, looking about nineteen again. And for a split second Andie could almost believe they had gone back in time, that her dreams had come true and she and Conn were together as they'd once promised to be.

She shook the illusion off impatiently and pointed down through the trees to where she could see a glint of blue. "I see water—and a picnic table. But it doesn't look very sheltered."

"I have a feeling that Plan A is going to have to be scrapped." Conn nodded at the sky. "We're not in the clear yet, darlin'." A rumble of not-too-distant thunder seemed to agree with him. "I suggest we execute Plan B."

"That being?"

"That we hightail it to the other side of the lake. The lodge has three rental cabins over there that they use during hunting and ski season. We can take cover in one of them until the rain blows over."

"If it blows over." She was looking back at the turbulent clouds rolling ever closer.

"It will," Conn replied easily. "Trust me, darlin'." He tugged the mare's head around and poked her in the ribs with his heel to get her moving. "But the closer those clouds get, the better Plan B is starting to look."

"I second that." Andie gave the sky one last doubtful look, then nudged the chestnut along the narrow, winding trail that led down through the trees toward the lake.

Andie felt the first drop of rain a few minutes later, just as they cleared the trees and came into the open beside the lake. It hit her cheek, a big, lazy splash of cold water that made her blink, and she looked at the darkening sky warily.

But once she got a good look at Wolf Lake, she forgot about the rain. The south flank of Wolf Mountain towered above them, its top wreathed in cloud, a wall of sheer rock sweeping straight down to disappear into the crystalline depths of the still, deep lake lying at its feet. The other three sides sloped gently down to the water, ablaze with wildflowers and dotted here and there with clumps of cottonwood and tall pine trees.

The setting looked like a postcard, but even as Andie gazed at the scene, spellbound, a sudden breeze riffled the water's surface and the reflected mountains and clouds shimmered and vanished. And then, abruptly, it was raining. Huge drops of icy water pattered around them, making the horses snort and dance, and Andie glanced at the sky again. It was a solid sheet of roiling, black cloud, and a thin, cold wind had picked up, moaning through the trees. Lightning flickered behind them, and a moment or two later the valley shook under the rolling surf of thunder.

It died to rumbling echoes, and Andie gave Conn an eloquent look, saying nothing.

He just grinned at her, the wind ruffling his tousled dark hair. "Not to worry, darlin'. I've got it covered. Just keep thinking about that Triple-Threat Chocolate Surprise."

A gust of wind dashed a handful of chilly rain square into Andie's face and she swore breathlessly, battling the gelding as he tried to turn back up the path. Ears flattened, he fought the bit, but she got him turned onto the path that meandered along the edge of the lake. She urged him into a fast canter as a rumble of thunder rolled down the valley and another sharp gust of wind whipped across the lake, making the tall pines sway and moan.

There was another crack of thunder, this one sharp and close, and the gelding didn't need Andie's urging to break into a gallop. It was raining in earnest now, a hard, slashing rain that was cold enough to take Andie's breath away, and she tucked her head down as the gelding pounded down the path.

And then, with no warning at all, he went out from under her and she was cartwheeling over his head.

She landed flat on her back with a thud that practically jarred her teeth loose, and she lay there, breathless and stunned, as the cloud-roiled sky spun gently above her. She was vaguely aware of the gelding lunging to his feet, one shoulder and flank smeared with mud and grass. Of another horse careening to a stop right beside her, shod hooves flashing. Of someone looming above her, kneeling beside her, shouting at her through the rain and wind.

Conn.

She squinted against the rain falling in her eyes and managed a rough smile. "Did I win?"

"Nah. Not even close." Conn was on his knees beside her, his face white. "You only did one full turn before you hit dirt. I still beat you—that day I got thrown, I did a double cartwheel."

"Maybe next time." Still badly winded, she closed her eyes. "Man, that hurts."

"Damn it, Andie—" His voice vibrated with worry. "Don't move, all right? Just don't move until—"

"I'm okay." Managing another weak grin, she opened her eyes and started to sit up. "Nothing's broken."

Rainwater was sluicing down the neck of her jacket, soaking into the sweater and blouse beneath it, and she shivered violently. "Is the horse all right? Is he okay?"

Two strong hands grasped her shoulders and pushed her gently back against the sopping wet grass. "Quit worrying about the damned horse. The horse is fine. Quit flailing around and—"

"Connor, I'm all right. Or will be if you'd let me sit up— I'm drowning, lying here like this!" She pushed his hands aside and struggled into a sitting position, head swimming. "I'm okay. Just need to catch my breath...."

Conn slipped his arm around Andie's shoulders to support her, trying to shelter her from the pelting rain with his own body as she sat huddled there, looking pale and dazed. "Damn it, Andie, you scared the hell out me," he got through gritted teeth, his heart still hammering. "I thought you'd really done it this time, lady."

"I'm okay."

She shivered again and Conn pulled the collar of her jacket tight around her throat. He brushed a handful of soaking hair gently from her face with his free hand, cradling her against him, and looked around them. It was raining even harder now, that kind of heavy rain that showed no signs of letting up anytime soon, and he swore under his breath.

This was all his fault. If he hadn't been so intent on keeping Marc Beck away from her, they'd both be down in the lodge right now, sitting in front of a crackling log fire drinking brandy, warm and dry. If she'd been hurt...

Conn hugged her against him as tightly as he dared, closing his eyes for a shaken moment. If she'd been hurt, he'd never have forgiven himself.

"M-maybe we'd better get going," she said through chattering teeth. "We're getting soaked out here, and a piece of that Triple-Threat Chocolate Surprise would go down really good about now."

Conn managed a rough laugh, giving her a fierce hug and burying his face in her soaking hair. Even the thought of a world without Andie in it chilled him to the bone. Never again having her razz him about something, never again seeing that slow, mischievous smile tilt her mouth to one side, never again turning around at times during his day and just seeing her there....

Gently he eased back on his heels to look down at her, squinting against the rain. "Do you think you can ride?"

All his concern got was an impatient look. "Of course I can ride. I'm just a little winded, not mortally wounded."

"You came down like a sack of cement. You might have done more damage than you think, and I don't want you to—"

"Thanks a lot." She gave her head a shake and sprayed water in all directions. "Like a sack of cement! I've seen you make some pretty ungraceful dismounts in your time, mister."

In spite of himself, Conn had to smile. She didn't *sound* hurt. In fact, she sounded pretty normal.

A flicker of jagged lightning creased the sky and they both ducked instinctively, wincing as the thunder cannonaded around them a split second later, a crashing explosion of noise so loud, it made Conn's ears ring.

"Oh, damn!"

Andie grabbed his arm suddenly, eyes wide, and Conn felt his heart turn over. "What? Andie, what is it? Are you—?"

"Conn—the horses! Quick—catch the horses!"

Conn looked over his shoulder in time to see the two horses wheel around and bolt up the path, eyes rolling with fear, reins and stirrups flying.

Swearing ferociously, he lunged to his feet, taking two strides after them before realizing it was useless. He watched them disappear into the lashing rain and mist and swore again with enthusiasm, raking his dripping hair out of his eyes.

"I suppose," Andie said calmly, "that our Triple-Threat Chocolate Surprise was in one of those saddlebags."

"You got it," Conn growled. The rain pounded down across his shoulders, plastering his denim shirt to his skin, and he could feel it running down his ribs like small cold fingers. He looked around at Andie, finding her on her feet. "How do you feel?"

"Wet." She grinned at him, then bent down stiffly to retrieve her camera case from a puddle of muddy water. "What now, Tonto?"

"The cabins are just down there." Conn nodded toward the lake, squinting into the rain. It was coming down harder than ever now, the wind lashing the small, bitterly cold drops into a stinging curtain. He reached for Andie's hand and her small fingers folded around his. "Run . . . !"

Skidding on wet leaves and sheets of glistening, slippery rock, they raced through the pelting downpour, Conn half dragging her as they hit level ground. A small log cabin appeared from out of the mist and rain and they hit the door at a dead run, staggering into the dim shelter, helpless with laughter.

"I don't believe this!" Conn slammed the door closed on the storm, still laughing. Rainwater sluiced off him, soaking the pine floor, and he gave himself a shake. "Sorry, darlin'. I guess this whole picnic idea was a bad one all around."

Andie plucked at her soaking wet jacket, wrinkling her nose expressively. "Well, I'll admit the special effects could use some work. But—" she started wringing water out of her hair "—the picnic was a great idea."

Conn gave a snort of laughter. "Aside from the fact we're half-drowned and stranded in the middle of nowhere and our lunch went south, you mean."

"Details, details." She grinned up at him, licking rainwater from her lips. "Come on, Devlin, lighten up! We've been wet before. Heck, we've even been stranded before. Remember the time you, Joey Michaelson and I went camping up near Mount Saint Helens? We got separated and Joey thought we'd caught a ride home with someone else and he left us there. And as for our picnic lunch..." She shrugged. "Well, that Triple-Threat Chocolate Surprise was probably overrated anyway."

"Probably." Conn slipped his arm around her shoulders and gave her a hug. "You're a good sport. Either one of my ex-wives would have had my head—or worse—on a stake by now." He shrugged out of his jacket and hung it over the back of a wooden chair where it dripped noisily.

Andie shivered violently, looking around the small cabin. It was small and rustic but comfortably furnished with a couple of big Colonial chairs and a sofa grouped around a big stone fireplace. Two big oval, braided rugs covered the pine floors, and a simple pine table and four matching ladder-back chairs sat in one end of the room beside a big window that overlooked the lake. A tiny galley kitchen was tucked in one corner, separated from the rest of the room by an island counter, and in the opposite corner was a set of bunk beds with bright red spreads.

"I'll get a fire started," Conn said from behind her. "How about checking to see if that lantern on the table has any kerosene in it? That looks like a package of matches beside it."

Andie nodded mutely, gritting her teeth to keep them from chattering. She gave the lantern a shake, relieved to find it almost full. Fumbling with the waterproof package of matches, she finally managed to get one out and strike it. The wick caught after a moment and she replaced the chimney, turning the flame down until it stopped smoking. The warm glow seemed to shove the shadows and chill back a bit, but it was still cold and she shivered again.

Hugging herself, she walked over to stand by the fireplace. Conn was busy with kindling and a crumpled ball of yellowed newspaper, peering into the grate with a frown of concentration. Flame flickered to life, growing, and he fed it a few sticks of dry kindling.

He gave a grunt of satisfaction. "That's got it. It'll start to warm up pretty soon."

Andie just nodded again, huddling as close to the crackling flames as she dared, fighting the racking shivers as a pool of water grew around her feet. Her hair drooled down the back of her neck and she moved aside stiffly as Conn got to his feet.

Conn rummaged through various kitchen cupboards until he found a kettle, and he put it under the one tap above the small sink, not really expecting there to be water. But to his surprise it came out with a gush, a little rusty at first but then as clear as crystal, straight from the lake and as cold as ice.

The old wood stove took longer to get going. The rest of the kindling was damp, and it took a couple of tries to get it to burn, but he coddled it until it caught properly. Then he carefully stacked on a couple of dry logs and closed the cover, adjusting the flue to get a good draft.

Andie was still standing by the fireplace where he'd left her, arms wrapped around herself, looking miserable and cold. A quick search of the storage cupboards uncovered a stash of big towels and a couple of blankets, and he carried them across, dropping a towel around her neck and tossing the blankets on a nearby chair.

"How are you doing?" He started gently toweling her wet hair, feeling her shiver. "You look like that spaniel pup I hauled out of the river when I was fifteen."

"I'll live," she mumbled through towel and wet hair.

"Okay..." He gave her hair one more rub, then stepped back and eyed her thoughtfully. "Strip."

"You wish." Still shivering, Andie started rubbing her hair with the towel. "I'll dry out in a few minutes."

"In a few days, maybe." Conn had to smile. "Come on, Andie, get 'em off or I'll take 'em off for you. You're soaked to the skin and half-frozen on top of it. There's a time for maidenly modesty, but this isn't it."

"Is this the line you use on all the women you take to lunch?" She glared up at him through a tangle of wet hair.

"Only the good-looking ones." He grinned down at her, thinking idly that even soaking wet, with her hair plastered down and not a speck of makeup in sight, she was still gorgeous.

Funny, how he took that for granted sometimes, seeing her but not really *looking* at her. Not the way a man usually looks at a gorgeous woman. Not the way Alain De-Rocher and Marc Beck had been looking at her.

Frowning, he reached out and pulled her jacket off her shoulders, then grabbed the lower edge of her blue sweater and tugged it up. "Lift your arms."

She lifted them obediently and he pulled the sweater over her head and tossed it aside, but when he reached out to undo the top button of her blouse, she slapped his hand away. "I'll do it."

"Chicken." Grinning, he turned away from her and started unbuttoning his shirt. He stripped it off and draped it over the back of a chair, then started rubbing his arms and shoulders dry with another towel. "Tell me when you're decent."

Andie dabbed at a trickle of water wandering down her cheek, staring distrustfully at Conn's broad, muscled back. She shivered again suddenly, then tossed the towel aside with a resigned sigh and started to peel out of her blouse and soaking jeans. Even her bra and panties were soaked through and she stood there for an indecisive moment, then peeled them off, too, deciding that Conn was right about there being a time and place for modesty.

She rubbed herself with the towel until her skin glowed, then wrapped one of the blankets around herself and knotted it firmly, hanging her dripping clothes over the edge of the woodbox. The fire crackled comfortably and Andie could already feel the chill in the room starting to lift. Combing her hair back with her hands, she turned to tell Conn that he could turn around now.

And instead just stood there with her mouth half-open, transfixed.

He was standing with his back to her, whistling softly, as naked as the day he'd been born. His jeans and briefs lay in a sopping pile on the floor beside him and he was toweling his torso dry.

Powerless to help herself, Andie watched as the lamplight played over the contours of his rain-damp body. She'd forgotten how well proportioned he was, broad-shouldered and lean-hipped, with long, well-muscled legs and the grace and economy of movement of the natural athlete.

He half turned toward her, glancing up and catching her stare. Completely unembarrassed, he straightened and calmly draped one of the blankets around his hips, nodding toward the stove. "I'll see if I can scrounge up some tea or coffee or something."

"I, um . . . will help you." To her annoyance, Andie felt a hot blush spill across her cheeks and she turned away and walked toward what looked like a pantry cupboard, furious at her childish reaction to an innocent situation.

Wishing her cheeks would stop burning, she fumbled with the animalproof catch on the cupboard, finally managing to get it undone, then wrenched the door open.

There was nothing inside but a few big metal canisters, but when she pulled one of them toward her, she realized it was full. It took a minute to pry the tightly sealed top off, but when she finally got it open and peered inside, she gave a mutter of satisfaction. "Well, we won't starve, anyway."

"What did you find?" Conn appeared beside her suddenly, his bare arm pressing against her shoulder.

"Soup mixes—three, four, five different kinds. Dried vegetables. Beans. What's this?" She pulled out a bag and peeked inside. "Lentils."

"Powdered milk." Conn had opened one of the other canisters and was rummaging through it. "Sugar. Flour. Rice."

"Hot-chocolate mix. Tinned milk." Andie was rifling through the smaller tins stacked on a lower shelf. "Baked beans. Chili—Texas-style, extrahot. That sounds like it has possibilities." She pulled the heavy tin out and set it aside. "Some tinned veggies. More soup."

"Pasta."

Andie reached for another big canister just as Conn did and his forearm brushed against hers, their hands colliding. The sensation of his bare skin against hers sent an odd little tingle through Andie, almost like an electric shock, and she drew her arm back self-consciously. "Sorry. Go ahead."

She swallowed, feeling silly and awkward for some reason, vibrantly aware of how close he was standing, of the warmth radiating off his bare chest, the scent of his rain-damp skin.

As he pulled the lid off the canister, his arm touched hers and he left it pressed against her, warm and damp. "Tea. Coffee."

Conn's voice sounded oddly tight and she glanced up at him just as he looked at her and as his gaze hit hers, Andie felt another little tingle shoot through her. There was something in his eyes that made her breath catch slightly, an awareness she'd never seen there before—awareness of *her*, not just as Andie, but as a woman. Awareness of himself. Of the fact they were alone up here, half-naked and surrounded by firelight and storm.

A flood of memories hit her—memories of making love with him in a cabin much like this one. Vital, vivid memories of exactly what it had been like: the slick whisper of flesh on flesh in the firelit shadows that night, the way he'd filled her, heavy, solid, male. The weight of his body on hers, more erotic than anything she could remember. The things she'd seen in his eyes as he'd moved within the tender prison of her body.

The package of soup mix she'd been holding hit the floor with a thump and she started slightly. She managed to tear her gaze from Conn's, breathing unsteadily, and she reached up to brush her damp hair off her cheek in a nervous gesture she caught halfway through. "I... Soup would be nice. Don't you think?"

"Yeah." His voice was rough and he sounded distracted, as though soup was the last thing on his mind. "Soup'll be fine."

But she made no move to pick up the package of soup and neither did Conn. Made no move to turn away, and neither did Conn. There was a crash of thunder that made the windowpanes rattle, but she barely noticed, aware of nothing but the rhythmic beat of her own heart, the heat from Conn's bare arm, the sound of his breathing.

And then, for no reason at all, she found herself turning toward him, lifting her head to look up at him. And wasn't even surprised to find his mouth just *there*, touching hers, lips brushing hers lightly, no more pressure than the warmth of his breath. She let her eyes slide closed and put her hands out to steady herself, palms resting on his bare ribs, and he settled his hands on her shoulders, fingers curling lightly around the back of her neck, warm and strong, yet so gentle it was almost a caress.

His mouth made another pass across hers, barely touching, the tip of his tongue caressing her lower lip. Her lips parted of their own accord and he kissed her very gently, just a brief pressure of his mouth on hers, tongue sliding between her lips then away before she was even fully aware of it. His lips closed gently on her lower one for an instant; then he touched the bow of her upper lip with his tongue again, a silken caress that made her shiver.

Lightly, she ran her fingertips up his chest, brushing the hard nub of his nipple and hearing his breath catch ever so slightly, nails catching in the wiry hair as she slid her fingers slowly through it. Wanting, needing to touch him. Tasting the heat of his breath on her mouth and wanting more, touching his lips with the tip of her tongue, feeling them part. Daring to kiss him lightly, letting her mouth rest on his, sliding her tongue along the cleft between his parted lips and finding his there... the first teasing touch, silk on silk, headily erotic.

Too erotic. It made her dizzy and confused, and she turned her head away, let it drop forward until she was resting her forehead on his wide chest, eyes closed, feeling shaky and suddenly very warm. Wondering what was happening. Why he was letting her do this, why she was letting herself do this....

His fingers caressed the side of her throat, then her shoulders, and she could feel the warmth of his breath on her ear, her throat. And then, finally, he drew his hands lingeringly from her shoulders and stepped back from her.

"Vegetable okay?"

She drew in a very deep, careful breath. "Yes," she whispered, not even daring to look at him. "Fine. That's fine."

And then he stepped away and was gone, the air suddenly chill again, and Andie took another deep breath and looked around. He was standing by the sink, frowning a little as he read the directions on the package.

"I think—" Her voice was so hoarse, she had to swallow. "I think all you have to do is add boiling water."

"All right." He looked at her then, and even from across the room it was like a physical touch, his gaze holding hers for a long, taut moment.

Then he smiled slightly, just a hint of lazy acknowledgment that he was as aware as she that something had happened in the past few minutes that was catching them both by surprise. Was still happening even as he stood looking at her. Could evolve into something else again should they both agree to it.

The smile widened and his eyes warmed, locked with hers. Then he turned away and started looking through the cupboards as though nothing had happened at all.

Eight

Andie stood there awkwardly for a minute or two, not quite knowing what to do. She didn't want to get dressed again. Just the thought of putting on those sopping wet jeans and blouse made her shudder. But she wasn't certain that staying wrapped up in nothing more substantial than a scratchy wool blanket was what she wanted to do, either.

Then she finally just padded across to the fireplace, too confused at the moment to know what she wanted, other than to get warm and dry. Her leather camera case was lying on the coffee table where Conn had dropped it, and she picked it up and carried it across to the fire, shaking muddy water from it. She sat down on the braided rag rug, as close to the fire as she could get without actually singeing herself, and opened the case to check her camera and film.

Conn heard Andie swear and glanced around in time to see her snatch up something from the rug and stuff it back into her camera case. "Is your film still okay?"

"What?" She looked up at him, cheeks pink from the fire's heat, and stared at him. Then she blinked. "Oh. Yeah. The film's fine." She smiled slightly and closed the case, setting it on the hearth. "I'm just going to kill Tracy, that's all."

"Again?" He had to laugh. "What did she do this time?"

"Got in the last word, as usual."

"What about?"

But Andie shook her head, letting her gaze drop, and wrapped her arms around her upraised knees and tugged the blanket more tightly around her. "Nothing important."

Conn just nodded, then went back to what he was doing. The box of biscuit mix he'd found made it sound easy, but he was starting to have his doubts that they were going to have fresh baked buttermilk biscuits with their soup. Another minute or two, in fact, and he was going to toss the whole mess out.

But then it looked as though it was going to work out after all, and he dropped mounds of biscuit dough into a baking dish he'd found, shoved it into the oven and hoped for the best.

To his profound surprise, he opened the oven a few minutes later and discovered that he hadn't done half badly at all. They were lumpy-looking things, and a couple of them had scorched, but all in all they looked edible. And if smell was anything to go by, they might even be good.

Pleased with himself, he dumped soup mix into a couple of mugs and poured boiling water on top of it, tossed the biscuits into a small wicker basket he'd discovered in the top cupboard, added the tinned butter he'd found, put the whole works on a tray that had been on the counter and carried it in to where Andie was sitting by the fire.

Andie was staring into the flames and she looked up when he came in. Her eyes met his and Conn felt his gut tighten, that little sizzle of sexual awareness between them still there.

She felt it, too, and let her gaze slide from his. Conn eased out a tight breath and set the tray on the stone hearth, telling himself it was nothing he couldn't handle. Just a few stray sparks left over from that morning in his house, that was all. The storm. The fire and lamplight. Knowing she was deliciously naked under that old plaid blanket she had wrapped around her. Knowing one tug on that knot was all it would take...

He wrenched his thoughts back into line and dropped onto the rag rug beside her, forcing himself not to notice the way the firelight spilled down the silken curve of her shoulder. "This isn't what I planned for this afternoon," he said gruffly, "but it's hot."

"And biscuits." Her voice was rough. "How did you manage that?"

"Read the back of the box."

"Oh." She picked up one of the mugs and took a cautious sip of the steaming hot soup. "It's good."

"When I promise a lady a picnic, she gets a picnic."

She nodded again, still not quite meeting his eyes, and Conn found himself noticing for the first time in years that she still had freckles. Not many, but they were still there, scattered across the bridge of her nose just the way they'd done twenty-odd years ago. She'd always hated them, he recalled suddenly.

"Lemon juice."

She'd been tearing a hot biscuit in half and stopped, looking at him questioningly.

Conn had to laugh. "I was just remembering that summer when you were about fourteen, and you kept rubbing lemon juice on your freckles to bleach them out."

"What on earth made you think of *that?*"

"You still have a few—here." He reached out without even thinking and ran the tip of his finger across her cheek, his gut pulling a little tight at just that innocent a touch. Very carefully, not sure what was going on but knowing it could get him into trouble, he drew his hand back.

Andie had gone very still. He could see the pulse in her throat and found himself staring at it, fighting a sudden urge to lower his mouth to that exact same spot and—

"This is nice."

Andie's voice sounded a trifle breathless and Conn tore his gaze from her throat to meet hers. "The soup?"

"The picnic." She looked away again after a moment, tearing off another piece of biscuit although she hadn't tasted the first bit yet. Then she glanced at him, smiling. "It *was* a good idea, Devlin. And I apologize for the hard time I've been giving you lately. I keep forgetting you're newly divorced and not quite back to normal yet."

Conn managed a humorless smile. "So do I. Judith and I were separated for so long that by the time the actual divorce came through, I had a hard time remembering I'd ever been married to her."

"Do you think you'll try again? Getting married, I mean?"

Conn blew out his breath, thinking about the question. "I don't know," he finally said. "I'd still like some of the things that being married means—loving someone, having someone love you. Kids." He frowned slightly. "I'd like kids."

"Me, too."

Her voice sounded subdued, and Conn glanced at her, finding her staring into the fire. It made him frown, thinking of Andie and children. He'd never thought of it before. Had never considered her as a wife and mother. "Is that why you're thinking of marrying DeRocher?"

She blinked, as though startled out of a daydream. "Yes. Yes, I suppose that's part of it. And the other things you mentioned. The loving. The being loved."

"*Do* you love him?" He asked it bluntly, watching her face.

"Of course. I wouldn't marry him if I didn't love him, would I?"

But it was a lie; Conn knew it even as she was saying it. Anyone else would have missed it. But he knew her too well. "And Marc Beck. What's he? Just a distraction?"

Andie's head came up, her eyes suddenly cool. "You know me better than that, Connor."

He winced slightly, suddenly feeling like a fool. "Yeah, I do. I'm sorry."

She nodded after a mistrustful moment, looking only partly mollified. "I could ask you the same question about Olivia Woodruff."

Conn had to chuckle. "Now *there's* a distraction!"

"If you like silicon."

Conn gave her a startled look. "Like hell!"

Andie's mouth curved up in a gentle smile. "Perhaps. But she seemed pretty knowledgeable when she said she could put me in touch with a cosmetic surgeon who, as she put it, 'does spectacular boob jobs.'"

"She said that?" Conn blinked. "To you?"

Her smile widened slightly. "Mmm. I guess she thinks I'm a little flat-chested."

Conn gave a grunt of thoughtful consideration, eyeing Andie's front with more than normal interest. "I don't see anything the matter with your chest. In fact, I've always figured you had a pretty nice chest."

"And coming from a man who knows chests, I consider that a compliment."

"Are you saying I like big-breasted women?"

"I'm saying you just like women, period."

He thought it over. "Guess I can't argue with that. God knows, I've married my share."

"More than your share," Andie said with a snort.

There was more truth than humor to the words, but Conn threw his head back and let loose with a belly laugh, the first he'd enjoyed in a long, long time. It felt good, washing away some of the moody glumness that seemed to hang over him lately. "Can't argue with that, either," he said, still laughing.

Too bad marriage couldn't be more like *this,* he thought. Sitting in the firelight laughing over old times, relaxed and comfortable, each knowing the other so well he didn't even have to finish his thoughts half the time. Too bad he couldn't marry his best friend....

As before, he found himself just watching her. Never noticing until now how graceful her hands were, the fingers long and slender. Or the curve of her bare shoulders, burnished by firelight, the skin glowing like smooth satin. Or the soft swell of her lower lip... He stared at that lip, thinking that she had the most kissable mouth of any woman he'd ever known—sweet and warm and responsive.

There was a tiny crumb there now, and he reached out and cradled her chin with his fingers and brushed the crumb away with his thumb. Slowly. Loving the feel of her mouth as he traced its curve with his thumb again, outlining her upper lip, then down to the moist cleft between.

Her lips parted and he felt the delicate touch of her tongue against his thumb and watched, heavy-lidded, as she took it into her mouth, her eyes locked with his. And it was then, in that heartbeat moment that seemed to last an eternity, that Conn realized they'd been heading for this moment all day.

He took his thumb from between her lips and traced her lower lip again, and then, slowly, knowing there was no rush whatsoever, he lowered his mouth to hers and kissed her slowly.

She didn't seem to be any more surprised by it than he was, lips already parting in welcome, greeting the probing touch of his tongue with hers. Her hands touched his bare shoulders delicately, almost tentatively, one running up through his still-damp hair, the other curling around the back of his neck.

He drew his mouth from hers finally, laughing, and brushed her hair back from her face to gaze down into her eyes. "We said this sort of thing wasn't going to happen."

"I know." She traced his face with her eyes, feature by feature, as though she'd never really seen it before. "This is crazy."

"Damn right." And then he was kissing her again, seriously kissing her this time, just letting himself go with it, losing himself in the sweet magic of her. It felt right...God, anything that felt this good had to be right!

"We probably shouldn't be doing this," she murmured against his mouth a minute or two later, her mouth browsing along his lower lip.

"I agree. Absolutely." He lowered his mouth to her shoulder and caressed the soft skin with his lips, his pulse rate all over the map, willpower slipping badly. She smelled of rainwater and firelight, and he could feel the weight of her breast against his arm, the pressure of her thigh along his, and knew he was well on his way to losing it.

"Andie, I want to make love to you!" He groaned and turned his head away, knowing he should be pushing her away from him while he still had the strength. But then his mouth found hers and he was kissing her again, hard and deep, and knew it was already too late.

Andie opened her mouth fully to his, tasting his desire, hot and metallic, knowing she should be stopping him, that this was wrong, wrong, wrong. That she'd regret it in the morning. That, if they made love, working with him ever again would be all but impossible.

There were a thousand reasons—ten thousand reasons—not to let this go on...and yet she could no more have stopped him than she could stop the rain still hammering down on the shingled roof.

And then he was pulling her down onto the rug and the blanket she'd so modestly tied around her had fallen open and she was naked to him, her skin so sensitive that even the weight of his breath made her moan softly. The years dropped away and it was as though those twelve long years had never existed, as though they had made love just that morning, her body still remembering every touch of his hands and mouth.

"You're the most beautiful thing I've ever seen," he murmured, nuzzling her throat, her breasts, her belly. "How come we've never done this before, Andie?"

"We have."

"Long ago," he whispered, mouth moving, promising. He captured one taut nipple between his lips and teased it with his tongue. "Too long ago. I love your skin, like silk. Love the way you smell and taste and feel...."

She lifted his head and kissed him, thinking fleetingly that if she was ever going to say no, it had to be now. That this wasn't going to change things, that he wasn't suddenly going to fall in love with her and everything would be perfect. It was making love to her he loved, not her—not Andie, not his best friend. Nothing would be different afterward.

And yet, suddenly, she didn't care. For the moment he *did* love her, as deeply and passionately as any man had ever loved a woman. She was in his arms, and that was all that mattered. For now, anyway. And tomorrow...well, she'd deal with tomorrow when it arrived. Smiling a little, she slipped her arms around him and simply gave herself over to his magic.

And magic it was. He knew her by heart, a conquering hero retaking stolen lands; knew where to touch, and how, and just the right words to growl against her ear. Knew things she'd all but forgotten, the sly touch of his tongue, the caress of a fingertip, the exact way to coax sensations from her she'd never dreamed of having again.

He nudged her thighs apart gently with his, fingers gently teasing her, readying her, pleasing her—and then, suddenly, he went very still. "Andie..." He nuzzled the side of her throat, her ear. "Andie, tell me it's all right. Tell me you're taking something." He groaned, resting his forehead on her shoulder. "Please be taking something."

Andie's eyes flew open as she realized, finally, what he meant. For one insane instant she had her mouth open to say yes, that she was taking the Pill and everything was fine and they could make love, a tiny, tiny part of her thinking of what it would be like to have Connor's child. Of being able to fulfill even that small a part of the dream.

"Oh, Connor..." She closed her eyes, mind spinning, wanting him so badly, she was half out of her mind with it.

"Don't tell me." He tried to laugh, but it came out as a harsh groan. "Andie, Andie...this isn't what I want to hear!"

"My camera," she whispered, panting slightly, body so achingly ready for him she was trembling. "Get my camera."

Conn lifted his head and gazed down at her, his expression making her laugh out loud. "No, I'm not suggesting we just take pictures and forget the rest! There's—just hand me the camera case."

Obviously thinking she'd lost her mind, he reached around and picked up the damp leather case from the hearth.

"Open it. You'll find what you need...."

Still looking skeptical, he opened the case and peered inside. Then a slightly wicked grin canted his mouth to one side as he fished out one brightly wrapped contraceptive. "Should I even *ask* why you carry these in here?"

"It's a long story, but you can thank Tracy. She's the one who put them there, for reasons I'm not even going to start to explain."

"Tracy?" He looked surprised. "Little Tracy? Your kid sister knows about things like this?"

"My kid sister thinks she *invented* things like this."

"Ahh." He grinned, then lowered his mouth to hers and kissed her long and gently. "And here I thought I'd invented it."

"And here I thought," Andie said as she slipped her arms around his neck and tugged him back down against her, "that you'd just taken a good idea and made it better."

"I have an idea right now you might be interested in."

"I thought you might. And I think I am."

"Good." He gave a throaty laugh and started unwrapping the contraceptive. "How many of these do you have, anyway?"

"A handful. At least."

"That sounds like a challenge if I ever heard one," he murmured, easing himself between her thighs. "Could take all day, though."

"I have all day." Andie's breath caught. "Oh, Conn..."

"Then I suggest we get started," he whispered against her ear.

And did.

The last thing Conn was conscious of was hearing Andie give a low, throaty moan at the first intrusive touch of his body, and thinking a little insanely as he pressed downward and inward that making love to her was like coming home. And then there was nothing but hot silk and the sound of her sigh and an explosion of pure sensation as he made that first long, slow, slippery slide into ecstasy itself.

He moved gently and very, very slowly at first, wanting it to last forever, unable to even think of being anywhere but here, so deep within her they breathed with the same breath, felt the same heartbeat. She wasn't just his for the moment, but part of him, part of the fabric of his world, of everything that made him who and what he was.

She moaned again softly and he braced his arms and watched her with a kind of breathless wonderment as she arched under him, small white teeth across her lower lip as though to hold back a cry of pleasure, eyes closed. Her breasts lifted, the dark tips swollen, and the downy skin on her abdomen and belly glowed with firelight.

He drank in the sight of her loving him, unable to take his eyes from her as she lifted her hips to meet his downward thrust, the muscles in her belly tightening, her fingers clenching convulsively on his shoulders. Why in God's name hadn't they been like this all along? Why had he been searching for something that had been here from the beginning, looking for the semblance of love when he could have had the real thing?

He lowered himself over her again and cradled her head in his palms and she opened her eyes, and he read things there that took his breath away. Not saying anything, he simply smiled down at her and a moment later she smiled back and then he stopped thinking, stopped trying to figure it out, stopped trying to make sense of something that made no sense and just let himself go.

It didn't take nearly as long as he'd have liked, any plans he'd had of making it last gone after the first few minutes. It was hard and fast and good, and when he got there first, he was smart enough to just go with it, knowing she'd take longer, that they had plenty of time, that it would be better this way. He didn't rush it, but neither did he hold himself back, and when it finally happened, he just let it explode up and through him like a juggernaut, groaning her name with savage satisfaction.

And then, laughing a little at her first look of mild apprehension, he deliberately and slowly took her the rest of the way. She started to argue at first, saying it was all right, that she didn't mind, giving a shocked little gasp of surprise when she realized what he intended to do, blushing and embarrassed at the easy intimacies he was taking.

But then he reminded her it was hardly the first time, and that if you couldn't trust your best friend who *could* you trust, and that he was enjoying it almost more than she was . . . and after a distrustful moment or two, she let him love her the way he wanted to. And then she gave another indrawn gasp a moment or two later, this one of raw pleasure, and all her arguments were forgotten under his artful ministrations.

It took no time at all, his sly fingers and tongue finishing what his body had started, and she sobbed his name and tried to writhe away, but he held her firmly and watched her ride through it, up and over and down, crying out again and again as the spasms rippled through her.

Grinning a little, feeling fatuously pleased with himself, he eased himself up and along her trembling body and wrapped his arms around her, pulling her tightly against him. He could feel the tiny aftershocks still quivering through her and her heart hammering against his as she relaxed into his embrace, spent and dazed.

They lay like that for a long while, comfortable and relaxed, listening to the rain pound down on the roof of the cabin. He got up once or twice to poke the fire and add another log or two, then would stretch out beside her and pull the blanket over them. They made love again not too long afterward, this time slow and long, eyes locked, not saying a word until near the end.

Then he reared up onto his knees and lifted her across his lap so she was kneeling astride him, and she laughed and tangled her fingers into his hair and kissed him. And then she was loving him with wild, fierce intensity, her slender body moving like flame on him, uninhibited and joyfully greedy as she pleased herself again and again. And only then did she take the same ferocious joy in pleasuring him, taking a long, delicious time to make it so good for him that Conn had his doubts he'd be able to even move after it was over, let alone make love again anytime soon.

They spent the entire afternoon like that, storm forgotten, picnic and Devlin Electronics forgotten, everything in the world forgotten but the two of them and the small oasis of pleasure they inhabited. Andie got up once and made tea and rummaged around in the cupboards until she found a package of shortbread cookies. While she was doing that, Conn discovered that the sofa pulled out into a huge, soft bed.

He poked through the closet until he found extra sheets and blankets and an armful of pillows, and he made a deep, warm nest in front of the fire for them. Andie brought the tea and cookies over and they snuggled down against a pile of down pillows in a tangle of arms and legs, naked and warm and pleasantly tired, while the storm roared outside.

They got distracted after a while, and Conn set the tea and the rest of the cookies on the floor and turned to her with a glitter in his eyes that had nothing to do with the firelight. And in a little while he slid between her thighs and eased himself deep, deep into her welcoming warmth, in no hurry at all, each slow, lazy thrust of his hips just a prelude to the pleasures ahead.

They took their time, pausing now and again to catch their breath, shifting a little, trying something new, something old. Conn finally wound up half lying against a mound of pillows on his back with Andie above him, and he watched her through desire-slitted eyes as she lifted her arms and ran her fingers through her thick hair, back arched slightly, breasts lifted. She seemed in no rush, thighs clamped around his hips, her weight fully settled over him.

He'd planted his hands on her slender thighs, fingers splayed against the pale flesh, and he simply relaxed and watched her, loving the way the firelight flicked on her damp, warm skin as she moved, loving the shadows and curves of her, the thrust of her full little breasts, the whiskery weight of her pelvis astraddle his.

Her gaze met his just then and she smiled that Andie smile he knew and loved so much, and he found himself grinning back, knowing what she was thinking, knowing he didn't have to say a thing. It was like when they'd been kids and had practically been able to read each other's mind, knew now as then what she was thinking and feeling. Knew by the change in her breathing and the hunger in her eyes that she was getting closer, smiled again as he watched her take everything she needed, trusting him to let her do this, trusting him to help her, to know even better than she when it was time.

She caught her breath on a soft moan suddenly, lower lip between her teeth, her movements becoming uneven, almost urgent, and when he responded by starting to move under her at just the right moment, she moaned again and arched her back, thighs loosening. She seemed to shiver slightly and he moved his hand to where they were joined and started to caress her lightly and she sobbed something, clutching at his forearms for support.

He took her to the very edge of it and halfway over, and then very deliberately rolled over so she lay beneath him and finished it then and there, each strong, hard thrust of his body making her cry out with pleasure until finally it caught her and swept her away. She gave another sharp, startled cry, this one of pure satisfaction, and he followed it an instant later with one of his own. They collapsed, out of breath, panting into each other's arms, hearts hammering, and it occurred to Conn that he'd be perfectly content to stay up here with her for the rest of time.

They slept after that, tangled up in each other's arms in the fluttering shadows cast by the fire. Andie half wakened a couple of times and lay there in the half darkness, warm and sleepy, listening to the rain and watching Conn sleep beside her.

How easy it would be to convince herself that it could be like this forever. That from this day on she'd awaken every morning and find herself tucked close against him, thighs still gently aching from hours of lovemaking, and feel his breath on her cheek.

Too easy. In spite of herself, Andie smiled slightly. She knew it wasn't real. In a little while they were going to have to figure out how they were going to get back down to the lodge, and then Beck would be back and the negotiations for Becktron would continue and this brief magical interlude would be over.

She and Conn would share a day or two of secret smiles and promises to get together, but they never would. Back in the office, the magic would fade. She'd become Andrea Spencer again, administrative assistant and best friend, and things would be awkward for a day or two while they tried to figure out how to fit this afternoon into the real world. It wouldn't fit, of course, and finally they'd just let it go, savoring the memories now and again, maybe even teasing each other about it.

But it would have to end. He didn't love her, and they had no real future together. She couldn't just let herself slide into a relationship with Conn that consisted of easy sex and no commitment. She had too much pride for that. And it would hurt too much, being with him and knowing it was just a matter of time until he met someone he thought he loved and wanted to marry.

So...smiling, she reached out and touched his cheek with her fingertips, aching with love. Wanting him so badly she felt hollowed out and empty, coreless.

No delusions, she told herself fiercely, shutting her eyes tightly at the threat of spilling tears. And no regrets.

It was almost dark when she awakened again. The fire was snapping nosily, flames leaping, and she sat up sleepily and looked around. Conn was up, standing by the window at the front of the cabin, looking outside. He was still naked, firelight burnishing the planes and angles of his lean body, and she sat there for a silent moment, smiling as she watched him.

Only then did she realize how quiet it was. The fire crackled softly, but the rain had stopped.

"Has the storm blown over?" She shivered slightly and pulled the sheet up around her shoulders.

Conn glanced around, a smile tipping one corner of his mouth up. "Not exactly. You'd better come over here and see this yourself."

"Why? What's wrong?" Frowning, Andie slid from between the sheets, grabbing up a loose blanket and wrapping it around herself. "Jeez, it's cold in here!"

"I hope you weren't in any hurry to get back to the lodge."

Andie smiled as she walked toward him. "Not particularly. But we *should* start thinking about how we're going to hike down. It's a long way."

"Well, we're sure as hell not going anywhere tonight."

"Why?" She stepped beside him and looked out the window. "What—oh my *God!*"

Snow. The entire world had vanished under a thick blanket of snow. And it was still coming down, huge soft flakes spiraling out of the twilight sky like goose down. The trees were already covered with it, heavy boughs drooping under the weight, and the ground was nothing but a blanket of white. And it was silent, absolutely still; there was not even a breath of wind. Just the big tumbling flakes spilling down in a curtain so thick, she couldn't even see the edge of the clearing that led down to the lake.

"The temperature must have dropped while we were asleep," Conn said.

"What on earth are we going to do?" Andie looked at him, not quite frightened but decidedly uneasy.

"Stay in bed," was his reasonable reply. His grin widened lazily, eyes holding hers in a warm embrace. "You have a better idea?"

"Well . . ." She looked back out at the snow. "We can't stay up here forever."

"Someone will be looking for us. But not even the company copter can get through this." He reached out and slid his arms around her and tugged her against him. "We've got food, firewood and sex, darlin'. I can't for the life of me think of another damned thing we need." His mouth browsed along the nape of her neck. "With luck, it'll snow for a week."

"And Beck?"

"Beck who?" He nipped her earlobe, his hand making an interesting foray beneath the blanket, caressing her breasts with comfortable familiarity.

Andie smiled, relaxing against him, feeling his body already start to respond to the promise in hers. His hand slipped lower, then lower still, and she had to catch her breath at the sudden intimacy of his caress. She could see the room behind them reflected in the darkened glass, the flames flickering in the fireplace, the rumpled bed.

Breathing a little unsteadily, she watched their reflections as Conn deliberately tugged the blanket open, continuing to caress her, his hand moving slowly, erotically. Above her head, his reflection smiled a slow, knowing smile, watching her watching him.

"Want to go back to bed for a while?" His voice was just a husky purr, and his eyes glowed a little dangerously.

Andie wet her lips, already so aroused that it was difficult to breathe, wondering how it was possible to feel this way this soon. She should be exhausted, should never want to even think about sex again let alone some of the things she was thinking right now.

"Y-yes. Oh..." She shut her eyes and sagged against him. "Oh...please."

"So soon? I've barely even started."

"I know. Oh...I know! This...this can't be happening. It's impossible. Impossible."

And sometime later, dazed with sensation, listening to her own voice lifting through the stillness of the room in short, breathless cries of pure pleasure as Conn moved strongly and steadily in the hammocking cradle of her thighs, she discovered it wasn't impossible at all.

Nine

By dawn it had stopped snowing, and they awoke to a world so dazzling white, it took Andie's breath away. Her clothes were dry by then, or pretty much so, and she pulled them on hurriedly while Conn tried to coax the wood stove in the kitchen to cooperate long enough to boil water for coffee.

Pulling the cabin door open, she took a deep breath of crisp, cold air and laughed aloud, squinting against the brilliance. The sky had cleared and was so deeply blue, it hurt to look at it, and the snow was already melting, water pitter-pattering as it dripped off the eaves and drooping pine boughs and trickled down the path in a dozen noisy little streams.

She walked outside and turned her face up to the hot sun, thinking a little wistfully that it *would* have been nice if it had snowed for a week. Or at least a day or two longer.

She glanced over her shoulder at Conn, who'd gotten the stove going and was dumping coffee into an old percolator he'd found, whistling to himself. He'd pulled on his jeans but nothing else and was padding around in his bare feet, looking rugged and competent and just a little disreputable, hair tousled, lean cheeks sporting a fashionable morning-after stubble. One look at him and you knew what he'd been up to all night.

Grinning, she scooped up a handful of wet snow and sidled back into the cabin, trying to look innocent. Or as innocent as it was possible for a woman to look, she amended, after spending the rowdy night she had.

Conn glanced up at her and smiled. "So?"

"So, what?"

"So, how are you this morning?" His smile widened. "We haven't spent a lot of time talking since we woke up an hour or so ago."

"Oh, I'm just fine." She broke into a wide grin. "But I think you could use some cooling off."

Conn knew something was up the instant he looked at her, but it wasn't until the snowball hit him square in the chest that he realized what it was. He let out a yelp and leapt back, swearing, trying to paw it off him. He missed a lump and it went slithering down his belly and he swore breathlessly again as icy water trickled into his jeans.

Andie gave a whoop of laughter and Conn grinned, starting to slowly circle the end of the island and move toward her. "Not a good idea, darlin'. Not a good idea at all."

Still grinning, Andie started backing toward the door. "You're in your bare feet, Devlin," she reminded him quite practically. "I have my boots on. And you are *not* going to chase me outside in your bare feet."

"Try me!"

He made a lunge for her and she gave a yelp of laughter and bolted for the door, and Conn swore as she slipped out of his grasp like an eel and was outside before he could stop her. He was after her in the next heartbeat, not even bothering with shoes, and as she scampered across the veranda and down the stairs, he vaulted the veranda railing and caught her easily. Grabbing her around the waist with one arm, he intended to lift her up and carry her back inside, but he was off balance and the ground was slippery, and instead they both landed in a tangle of arms and legs in the nearest snowbank.

Conn got on top of her and held her hands, grinning down at her. "What were you saying about getting cooled off?"

"Connor! You're nuts! You're going to freeze your—"

"Say you're sorry, wench. Better yet, give me a kiss."

"Connor!" Half strangling on laughter, Andie wriggled and fought under his weight, then capitulated with a grin. "One kiss."

"Maybe two." He rested his mouth on hers, nibbling her lower lip. "On second thought, how about an even dozen?"

"We're going to get soaking wet again," she murmured, already slipping her arms around his neck.

"Then we'll have to take everything off and hang it up to dry," he whispered back, already starting to unbutton her shirt. "And stay in bed all damn day...."

"Better than staying out here all day... I'm starting to freeze!"

"I'll warm you up," Conn murmured, tracing a line of kisses along the upper swell of her breast. "I can think of at least a couple of—"

Andie had gone still, head turned slightly as though she was listening. "Conn, I hear something. Isn't that a—"

"Helicopter," he growled, turning his head to watch as the chopper came clattering up the valley, following the edge of the lake. "Hell." He blew out his breath and rested his forehead on her cheek, swearing again under his breath. "I think we just got rescued, darlin'."

Although it was too damn bad they couldn't have waited a day or two, he thought savagely, getting to his feet reluctantly. He reached down and tugged Andie up, then realized he was standing ankle-deep in melting snow and winced, making his way back to the cabin veranda.

The helicopter made a quick turn and came back, low enough that the downdraft from its rotors whipped up a froth of wet snow and lashed the pine trees, sending needles and small branches flying. It made a pass over the cabin and Conn lifted his arm in greeting, then let it drop by his side, wishing he could send whoever was aboard back down the valley for a day or two.

Instead, he simply watched it land with a fatalistic calm. It was the Becktron copter, and he wondered idly if Marc was piloting it. He glanced at Andie and grinned to himself. Too late, buddy. The best man *did* win.

But it wasn't Marc. The pilot was someone he didn't know, and the other two people aboard were Frank and Margie, both looking tired and frightened. Frank was out and running toward the cabin before the copter had even landed properly.

He grabbed Conn's outstretched hand in a ferocious grasp, then pounded him on the back. "Man, am I ever glad to see you two! You had us scared to death!"

Conn winced, realizing that he hadn't given a thought to the concern their disappearance might have caused. Andie, trying to hastily button her blouse and stuff it back into her jeans, gave him a quick guilty look, obviously thinking the same thing.

"We're okay. Andie's horse threw her, and when I was helping her up, they both bolted."

"I've never been so scared!" Margie's face was pale and she looked as though she'd been crying. "When the horses came down, we wanted to come up and look for you right away, but the lower trail was washed out."

"We called in the search-and-rescue people," Frank explained, "but by then it was snowing up here like there was no tomorrow and they couldn't send a plane or even a chopper up. We figured you'd found the cabins, but…" He gave his head a shake, his long homely face serious. "I'm telling you, Conn, you gave us all a bad night."

"We thought something terrible had happened," Margie said with a shudder. "All I could see was the two of you lying up here with broken necks, and then it started to snow."

Tears welled up in her eyes and Conn gave her a tight hug. "Hey, we're both okay. We got to the cabin before it started to snow. We're fine."

His eyes met Andie's over Margie's head and she bit her lip to hold back a smile, coming over to slip her arm around Margie's waist. "I feel awful," she said quietly. "You two spent the night worrying, and Conn and I—"

She stopped dead, mouth still open, and Conn grinned, interested in seeing how she was going to get herself out of the corner she'd just painted.

"We, um, we lit a fire and stayed warm and dry. And there was plenty of food." She glanced at Conn over Margie's head, and he gave her a quick, secret smile.

"Warm." Margie gave Andie, then him, a suddenly speculative look. Her gaze drifted past Conn and into the interior of the cabin, where the big rumpled bed—obviously the only one that had been used—was in plain sight. She nodded slowly, mouth warmed by the barest hint of a smile. "I see."

There was no need to remind her to keep it to herself, Conn knew. Margie had started working for him back when he and Billy Soames were still partners, and although she wasn't shy about giving him advice she thought he needed—including any about his love life—nothing she heard, saw or even speculated on ever went beyond the door of his office.

He just gave her a lazy smile, getting a mildly disapproving look in return. "I hope you realize what a scare you gave everyone," she said a bit tartly. "Up here keeping *warm* while the rest of us thought you'd fallen over a cliff and killed yourself. I think every television and radio station on the West Coast has someone on the story—the lodge is crawling with film crews and reporters."

Conn swore. "So much for keeping the Becktron buy-out a secret until we were ready to make an announcement."

"Desmond Beck's taking care of it. But the sooner you two get the rest of your clothes on and we get back, the better. There has been some interesting speculation going around." She looked at the two of them as she said it. "And I'm not just talking about the Becktron deal."

Conn swore again. "You're right. Let's move." A few minutes ago he'd have been happy to spend the rest of his life up here in bed with Andie. But now, abruptly, he was impatient to get back, wanting to get the negotiations with Becktron back in high gear and the deal signed. Wanting to get back to Devlin Electronics and see how things were going with those seismic units for DeepSix Exploration.

He strode back into the cabin, pausing long enough to take the now-bubbling coffee percolator off the stove before starting to grab up the rest of his discarded clothes. Andie came in behind him, looking a little pensive as she closed the door behind her. She looked across the cabin at him, not saying anything, then picked up her bra from the back of the chair where she'd hung it to dry.

As though suddenly shy, she turned her back as she slipped off her blouse and put on the bra. Conn watched her thoughtfully, wanting to say something to her, but not knowing what. Wanting to go across and slip his arms around her and tell her what it had meant, being up here with her. What making love to her had meant.

He suddenly realized that he didn't have a clue as to what she wanted to do now. Write the whole night off as a memory? A mistake? Continue their relationship when they got back to Seattle . . . ?

Hell, he hadn't thought about that. What *were* they going to do now? Yeah, he wanted to continue sleeping with her, but she might have an opinion or two about that. And there was that damned Frenchman to consider.

If they did get a relationship going, what then? Andie had always been his best friend, not his lover—what were the rules about sleeping with your best friend?

He swore and scrubbed his fingers through his hair, feeling more confused by the passing minutes. Damn it, none of this had seemed important last night. Drunk on sex, he hadn't been able to think further ahead than the next five minutes of pleasure.

Frowning, still thinking about it, he looked around to see if he'd forgotten anything. Andie's camera and its leather case were still sitting on the hearth and he picked them up, smiling. There was one condom left, believe it or not. He drew it out and toyed with it, giving Andie a speculative glance. They could tell Margie and Frank to go sightseeing for a half hour or so....

Then he shook off the whim and shoved the condom and the camera back in the case. Things were complicated enough already.

He walked across and handed the case to Andie. "Better hang on to this. Who knows when you might need it again."

You. He hadn't said *we* but *you,* Conn realized. He frowned, looking down at her, knowing he needed to say something. Anything, damn it. Just so she knew—

"Thanks." Her voice was emotionless. Almost cool.

And she still wouldn't look at him, Conn thought remotely. There had been none of her usual teasing, no laughter, not even a hint of warmth or tenderness. Nothing to indicate she even wanted to acknowledge what had happened up here. As though it was over and in the past and she'd prefer not to even mention it again.

She turned and walked toward the door, and Conn suddenly took a couple of long strides and caught her before she opened it. "Wait," he growled, pulling her around. "One last thing before we leave...."

She wasn't expecting it, and he felt more than heard her startled little intake of breath as his mouth landed across hers. He kissed her hard and long and deep, not getting much of a response, not really even expecting one. And when he lifted his mouth from hers a few moments later, he just grinned a little savagely. "God knows when I'm going to get the chance to do that again. It may have to hold us both for a while.''

There was something in her eyes he couldn't decipher, a soft tangle of emotions, and she simply gazed up at him, lips still softly parted, moist from his. Then she took a deep breath and nodded, frowning a little as she turned away. ''We'd better go.''

Conn frowned, too, wanting equally badly to stay. Wanting to scoop her into his arms and tumble across the bed with her and lose himself in her. Wanting . . . hell, wanting things he didn't even understand! ''We should talk.''

She gave him a quick, cryptic look, eyes searching his. ''We have to get back to the lodge, Conn.''

''Yeah.'' Smiling humorlessly, he reached out and brushed a tangle of hair behind her ear, her cheek like velvet against the back of his hand. ''Yeah, I guess we do.''

The small helicopter lifted off in a swirl of snow and dirt, and Andie relaxed finally as the pilot swung it around and they clattered down the valley, sunlight flickering off the rotors above them. She was jammed between Margie and Conn, and although Conn had wrapped his hand around hers, he seemed to be somewhere else, distracted and thoughtfully silent.

She was glad of the noise. It was a good excuse not to talk. She just wanted to get back to the lodge and have a long, hot shower and change her clothes and get back to work. She was bone tired—not surprising, considering she got precious little sleep last night. But most of all, she just wanted to be alone for a while.

She needed some time. Time to think. Time to figure out what she was going to do now. It was possible that Conn figured they were just going to continue sleeping together, and she had to sort through her feelings about that. And if he didn't, if he was going to take last night for the one-time magic it was, well...she had to figure out how to handle that, too.

They swung around the shoulder of Wolf Mountain and abruptly, the valley and lodge burst into view. The pilot headed for the parking lot where there was room to set down, and as they started to descend, Andie saw a flood of people pour out of the lodge and rush toward them.

"What on earth—?"

"I was afraid of this." Frank leaned across to peer out at the crowd of people. He looked at Andie and Conn. "Hang on to your hats, folks. This is where it gets interesting. These guys have been hanging around all night, waiting for some word."

Andie spotted the video cameras, bright with television network decals, and groaned. "Isn't there any *real* news for them to cover?"

"You two *are* real news," Frank said quietly. "When the president of Devlin Electronics disappears in a late-spring blizzard, that's news. When he *and* his second-in-command disappear, that's *big* news. Speculation ranges from accident to murder to a simple love tryst."

Beside her, Conn muttered a coarse oath, looking out at the news crews, some already filming the copter's descent. Frank got out first and tried to disperse the crowd pushing in with their cameras and microphones, but they ignored him, nearly running him down when Conn jumped down from the chopper, then turned to help Andie down.

"Hey, Mr. Devlin, is it true you're buying out Becktron?"

"Here, Miss Spencer. Look over here!"

Andie blinked, blinded momentarily by the sunlight, trying to turn away as someone shoved a microphone into her face.

"What was it like, being stranded in a snowstorm with the bachelor of the year, Miss Spencer?" A woman's face loomed in, eyes avid. "Are you and Connor Devlin lovers, Miss Spencer?"

Conn stepped between the woman and Andie. He dropped his arm around her and started pushing a path through the crowd. "Get out of the way, please," he said through gritted teeth. "Miss Spencer and I are fine, but we're tired and hungry. Someone from Devlin Electronics will be making an official statement later this morning. Now get the *hell* out of my way!"

Voices lifted in a storm of shouted questions, and Andie refused to look left or right as microphones and video cameras kept being shoved at her, staying close to Conn as Frank and Margie brought up the rear.

Desmond Beck was waiting for them inside the lodge, relief stamped all over his face. He greeted them warmly, then snapped out orders to a couple of his people, who immediately stepped in to stop the television crews and reporters stampeding through the big double doors.

Conn grabbed Andie's hand and they made their way up the stairs, the shouts and questions falling away behind them. And then they were inside her suite and Conn was closing the door, and all was silent.

"Well, I could have lived without that," Conn rasped, looking unamused. "You okay?"

Andie nodded wearily, tossing her still-damp jacket onto the sofa. "Yeah, I'm fine. I guess we should have realized this was going to happen. When word got out that you'd disappeared, it would have shaken up the entire electronics' industry. Your competitors would be praying you *had* gone over a cliff, and our suppliers and customers would have been praying you hadn't."

Conn gave a grunt, looking over the messages that had come in on the fax. *"Advise immediately whereabouts of C. Devlin pending cancellation of contract,"* he read out loud. "DeepSix Exploration." He glanced up at her, glowering. "Hell, do they think I'm making the damned things with my bare hands? Even if I had gone over a cliff, the contracts would be honored."

"Devlin Electronics *is* Connor Devlin, you know that."
She smiled and walked across to him. "You're a symbol,
hotshot—the American Dream, alive and well and living in
Seattle. Computer hacker makes good and all that."

"I was never a hacker."

"Oh? And what would you call someone who hacked his
way into the high school computer and gave himself a passing grade in English Lit?"

Conn winced. "God, aren't you ever going to let me forget that? I changed it back, for crying out loud."

"Only when I threatened to tell your dad."

He gave her a lazy grin. "Yeah, you always did keep me
on the straight and narrow. I was more scared of you than I
was of Dad *or* the principal."

"And so you should be."

"Hey." He reached out as she went to walk by him and
grabbed her around the waist, swinging her against him.
"What do you say we mess around for a while?" He nuzzled the side of her throat, his hands wandering with deft
familiarity. "We could get naked and spend the next hour
or so doing all sorts of things...."

She caught a marauding hand as it slipped under her shirt.
"Conn," she said a little breathlessly. "You have to have a
shower and change and finish the deal with Beck. And we
have to draft some sort of statement to keep the press happy.
And Mom—I have to call Mom to let her know I'm okay.
Ditto your parents. And take care of all these faxes and
everything."

Conn didn't say anything, holding her against him, his
warm breath curling around her ear. Then he swore very
softly and stepped away from her, his expression unread-
able. "You're right." Pulling off his shirt, he started walking toward the connecting door leading to his suite. "Call
Beck and tell him we'll get together in an hour. No point
wasting any more time."

Watching him disappear through the door, Andie sighed.
Maybe she should have just said yes and damned well let

Beck wait while she and Conn made love. For the last time, maybe.

Then again, maybe not. Groaning aloud, she ran her fingers through her hair, pulling it back. She was so confused!

Once back, it was as though they hadn't even been away. As though, Conn thought irritably a few hours later, he'd dreamed the whole damned thing. The ride into Wolf Lake. The storm. Andie. Just one more in the series of increasingly erotic dreams he'd been having.

They met with Desmond Beck for most of the afternoon, and by nightfall the deal was done. Becktron was his, save a few details yet to be worked out. He and Beck shook hands for the last time and then he stood near the doors of the lodge and watched the Becktron helicopter—*his* helicopter, now—lift off from the parking lot and vanish into the dusk.

Andie was still hard at work in one of the meeting rooms with some of Beck's people—*his* people—trying to get a handle on the best way to start merging the two companies.

It was a massive job, with months of hard and complicated work ahead, and it occurred to him as he walked wearily upstairs to his suite, that he'd hate to do this without her.

That steel-trap mind of hers had saved them hours of work today, cutting through the confusion of too many details, too much paper, seeing what was important and what could wait.

Andie. Just thinking about her made him smile. He thought of the small throaty sound of satisfaction she made when they made love. Of the scar on her inner thigh where she'd cut it open falling off her bicycle when she was nine. Of the way he'd kissed it last night, letting his mouth linger on the downy flesh there for a moment or two before going on to other, even more interesting places. Of the whispery little sigh she made when he did....

He had to stop this. Just thinking about it made him aroused and uncomfortable, and he jogged up the steps two at a time, laughing at himself. He hadn't felt this way in years, getting distracted at all the wrong times, thinking about sex when he should be thinking about business. Finding himself in the middle of a meeting and suddenly realizing everyone was looking at him, waiting for an answer, and he'd been so lost in a haze of erotic thoughts, he hadn't even heard the damned question.

Even now, he wanted to see her. Not just to skin her out of her clothes and wrap her long legs around him and make love to her until the sun came up—although God knows that was an idea!—but just to *see* her. Talk with her. Laugh with her. *Be* with her.

Hell, it was like being in love.

Still grinning, he unlocked the door to his suite and stepped inside, switching on the television as he walked by it, already unbuttoning his shirt. Some game show was in progress, and he ignored it as he pulled open the small bar. He poured himself a stiff shot of whiskey and tossed in a handful of ice cubes, then dropped onto the sofa and dropped his head back wearily.

"...and now the news," a voice from the television droned. "Millionaire playboy Connor Devlin, founder and president of Devlin Electronics, was found alive and unhurt this morning, after having been lost in the mountains near Timberwolf Lodge."

Conn threw his head up and glared at the television, the word *playboy* still ringing in his ears—and found himself staring into his own eyes.

It was a videotape, obviously taken as they'd gotten off the helicopter this morning. He swore savagely as he watched himself glower at the offending camera, heavily stubbled, hair uncombed, shirt still unbuttoned and hanging open, looking as though he'd just been caught in someone's bed.

The video was replaced by a still photo. It was a couple of years old, taken at a benefit he and Judith had attended, and his eyes narrowed now as he looked at it. He was dressed to the nines, looking impatient, and Judith was glaring up at him with enough venom to make him wince slightly even now.

"Twice married, self-styled renegade entrepreneur Devlin has made a reputation for himself for his kamikaze investment strategies, as well as for his fondness for marrying—and divorcing—beautiful women."

Two more pictures followed: he and Judith at their wedding, a snapshot of Liza taken not long after she left him.

"Found with Devlin was his assistant, Andrea Spencer." This accompanied by more of the video, and Conn swore again as he watched Andie get out of the helicopter, looking subdued and tired. "It has long been rumored that the relationship between Devlin and Miss Spencer goes well beyond business, though sources close to both deny this vigorously."

On the television screen, his alter ego was putting a protective arm around Andie's shoulder, guiding her through the crowd, holding her close. Too close, Conn thought. He should have been more careful. He shouldn't be putting Andie through all this because of *his* reputation as a womanizer.

There was a tap on the door connecting to Andie's suite and then the door was pushed open wide enough for her to stick her head in. She spotted the television and made a face, then pushed the door wider and came in. "So you already have it on."

"Bastards," Conn muttered. "A million real news stories out there, and they're wasting airtime speculating whether you and I are getting it off."

"You could always call up the station and tell them we are. Or did, anyway." Smiling comfortably, she came over and sat beside him, tucking her feet up. "That's a good picture of Olivia."

Conn's reply was short and profane as he watched the screen.

"Devlin, whose divorce from his second wife became final only this week," the woman anchoring the city desk was saying, "has been most recently linked with twice-divorced attorney Olivia Woodruff. Asked about her relationship with Devlin, Woodruff declined to answer."

"I didn't think she'd miss the opportunity," Andie said sweetly.

Grinning, Conn picked up the remote control and turned off the TV. Then he dropped his arm around her. "Want a drink?"

"Maybe later." She looked at him for a long moment, then leaned back and gave him a slow smile. "So. What now, hotshot? Do you take me to bed, or do we just shake hands and say thanks, it was great, and that's the end of it?"

Conn leaned forward to brace his elbows on his knees, rolling the glass between his palms. "Guess that's up to you."

"Am I to infer that means you don't have an opinion?"

"Oh, I have an opinion." He turned his head to grin at her. "Bed. That's my opinion." Then he let the grin fade and looked back at the glass, tipping it back and forth so the ice cubes rattled gently. "It could get complicated, Andie. Working together, sleeping together. Real complicated."

"Yeah. I know." She sounded thoughtful.

"And I'm scared of losing you." He glanced at her again, deadly serious now. "Sex has a way of making people crazy. If it starts to go wrong and you walk out like most of my other ladies have..." He shook his head. "I don't want to lose you."

She looked at him for a long while, eyes pensive. "Yeah, I guess there's that." Then she smiled faintly, reaching out to rub his shoulder. "Take me to bed, Conn. Make love to me. And in the morning, when we get back to Seattle, we'll just take things as they come, all right?"

It made him grin again and he got to his feet, pulling her up with him. "That's a hard offer to turn down." She came into his arms effortlessly, as though she belonged there, and he held her tightly against him and gazed down into her up-turned face, feeling something pull wire-tight inside him, making him a little dizzy. "Why the hell would you want to spend time with a worn-out, twice-divorced playboy millionaire like me, darlin'?"

Laughing, she leaned back in his arms and gazed up at him, her eyes as warm and inviting as an unmade bed. "I guess because I love you, you idiot. I always have. Isn't that reason enough?"

Conn smiled and lowered his mouth to hers, nibbling her lower lip. "Guess it'll do," he whispered. "Guess it'll do."

And much later, deep within the liquid fire of her, moving between her thighs slowly and rhythmically, feeling her respond, watching her respond, he felt that wire pull taut again, white-hot, catching a little in his chest.

She moaned very softly and tightened her thighs on his hips, shifting to take him even deeper, turning her head this way and that on the pillow and whispering his name in a breath-caught voice. He lowered his mouth and kissed her deeply and slowly, tongue sliding against hers in rhythms matching their lovemaking, feeling her shiver, tasting her desire as his own.

She moaned again and turned her mouth away, close now, so close... and he smiled, loving watching her when she simply let herself go like this, oblivious to everything but him and the pleasure he was giving her. Panting, she arched under him strongly, whimpering a little, hips flexing urgently, and he smiled again. Knowing what she needed. Knowing exactly how to make it perfect for her, even after just a handful of times.

He carried her through it and down, down the far side, finally letting himself go with the same abandon. And as it caught him in a dizzying explosion of pure sensation, he realized, very dimly, that this had to be the last time.

The last time.

Conn lay on his back, sheets kicked off, and stared at the ceiling. Beside him, Andie was sound asleep, curled up against him, her mouth lifted on a faint smile. He looked at her and reached out to brush her hair off her cheek, letting his fingers linger on her moist, warm cheek.

He'd made some mistakes in his life before, but none quite like this. What the hell had he been thinking, anyway?

Sex, that's what he'd been thinking. Like a damned stag in rut, that's *all* he'd been thinking. Him. It had all been about him.

But it was Andie who was going to get hurt. He'd do nothing but break her heart, just as he'd broken Liza's and Judith's. They'd both come to him thinking he was the man of their dreams, and look what had happened.

Twice-divorced playboy millionaire.

That was him, all right.

That was the real Connor Devlin, not the man Andie had let take her to bed up in the mountains. That was the old Connor, the one she'd grown up with and had shared a hundred adventures with. The one she thought she loved.

But there was no way he could be the man she needed and deserved. Hell, he had two ex-wives to prove he didn't know the first thing about commitment and love and making relationships work. If he led her on, if he let her think he was capable of giving more than he could, he was going to destroy everything between them. And he couldn't do that to his best friend. Even if he was halfway in love with her.

So it had to end. Here. And he had to leave her with no doubt whatsoever that she was better off without him in her life and bed.

Ten

―――――――

"You're going to *what?*" Andie simply stared at Conn blankly, deciding she'd either gone stone-deaf or flat-out crazy. Because there was quite simply no way he could have said what she'd thought he'd just said.

He looked at her from across his office, looking a little impatient at her apparent inability to understand plain English. "I said, I'm going to marry Olivia Woodruff."

Andie took a deep breath, then eased it out again quite calmly. Thought about it for a moment. They'd come down from Timberwolf that morning, and he'd been silent and grumpy the whole way, not saying more than four or five words, not looking at her. He'd dropped her off at her condo and she'd showered and changed, then had come down to the office . . . and now he was standing there telling her he was going to marry Olivia Woodruff.

"Connor, are you drunk?"

"No, I am not drunk." His eyes glittered slightly.

"Insane?"

"No." He bit it off.

"You can't be serious." She still sounded calm, she thought. Even rational. But inside she was screaming.

"Dead serious."

She drew in another careful breath, wondering if she could still be asleep and this was just a particularly nasty specimen of nightmare. "You cannot possibly marry Olivia Woodruff," she said very reasonably. "You don't love her."

"That's the best damned reason I can think of to marry her," Conn growled. His eyes held hers almost challengingly. "Look, Andie, I'm sorry. I know this weekend got a little out of hand, but—"

"Out of hand?" Her voice sounded almost too soft. Dangerous, even. "You spend most of the weekend making love with me, and all you can say is that it got a little out of hand?"

"Andie..."

"Tell me."

"Tell you what?"

"Tell me," Andie said through gritted teeth, "that I imagined the whole thing. That we did not make love—excuse me, have *sex*—about a dozen times in the past two days. That it meant absolutely nothing."

"You didn't imagine it. And it did mean something, damn it."

"Like hell it did! You didn't sleep with me because *you* wanted to—you slept with me because Marc *Beck* wanted to!"

Conn stared at her. "That's the craziest thing I've ever heard! What the hell kind of a man do you think I am?"

"That's why you can't stand the idea of me being with Alain, too. Not because you want me, but because you don't want *him* to have me. I'm like...like damned *property* to you! What are you going to do, make love to me once every decade just to keep your flag flying over me so no other man will dare even look at me?"

"Andie, we—"

"Don't!" So furious she was shaking, Andie clenched her fists at her sides, clinging to the fury for dear life. If the anger slipped even a little bit she'd fall apart, here and now and right in front of him, and there was just no way that was going to happen.

"Don't you *dare* hand me a bunch of morning-after platitudes like I'm just someone you picked up in a bar! I am not the flavor of the week, Connor Patrick Devlin. You do not spend a weekend in bed with me and then turn around and casually announce you are going to marry Olivia Woodruff and expect me to smile and step back and wait for another ten years to go by!"

Her voice nearly broke but she managed to catch it in time. "Not this time. Not *ever* again!" She wheeled around and stalked toward the door, so stiff, she was half afraid of shattering before she got there. She felt sick and numb to the bone, her mind spinning with disbelief and anger and a pain so great, it was like a deep surf sweeping over her.

"Andie? Andie—!"

But she was out the door and gone, snatching up her handbag from her desk and storming out, leaving a trail of slamming doors and astonished looks behind her.

To Conn's surprise, she was back in an hour. Looking calm and under control.

Maybe too calm, he decided warily, watching her through the open door of his office as she walked across to her desk and dropped an armful of packages she'd been carrying.

She took off her jacket and tossed it over the back of her chair, then turned and walked toward his office, giving him a cool look as she strode through the door. "Margie says you were looking for the production figures for the DeepSix Project."

She sounded brisk and no-nonsense, and he nodded even more warily. "Yeah."

Reaching across to a pile of papers stacked on the corner of his desk, she pulled a folder out, opened it and slapped it down on the desk in front of him.

Conn winced. "Sorry. Sometimes I can't see what's right in front of me."

"You got that right!" Turning on one heel, she stalked back toward the door.

He watched her as she sat down at her desk and started typing briskly at her computer, starting to feel uneasy for no reason he could pin down. God knows, she'd been mad at him before. Plenty of times. But there was something different this time. Something . . . final. Maybe he'd gone too far this time. Maybe he should have figured out a better way to handle it.

He was mulling this over, thinking about how he could start making amends, when she appeared at the door to his office again. She walked across with a sheet of paper in her hand, her face expressionless, and put it on the desk in front of him.

"I think this is all that's required. I've called Personnel and told them to get the paperwork ready. I'll sign everything I need to sign on my way out."

"Out?" Frowning, he glanced down at the paper she'd set in front of him, scanning it swiftly. Not understanding a damned word. Seeing only one thing . . . one single word that leapt out at him as though highlighted with neon ink. *Resignation.*

"What the hell's this?" He looked up at her.

"You can read. What does it look like? I'm quitting."

"You can't quit." He nearly laughed as he said it, the idea so preposterous, it had to be a joke. Her way of getting even with him.

Her eyes just held his, glowing with a deep anger he'd never seen before. "Yes, I can, Connor. And I am. Effective three weeks from today."

"Like hell, lady. Not with this Becktron deal in the bag. I need you."

"No. You *want* me, but you don't *need* me. I know you've never quite understood the difference, but you'll figure it out. Margie can handle whatever needs doing. As of now, I'm out of here."

"As of now?" He said it dryly, pushing the sheet of paper away from him. "I don't think so."

"I've got three weeks of vacation still coming, and I'm taking it." She smiled very slightly, but there was a distinct chill to it. "For a honeymoon."

He just stared at her, not smiling now. Knowing she didn't mean it, but not appreciating the joke. "Honeymoon."

"I bought my wedding dress. Would you like to see it?"

"Wedding dress."

"Invitations are going to be a problem though," she added conversationally, as though they were talking about what to have for lunch. "It takes about three weeks to get the engraving done, but I don't have three weeks. So…" She smiled. "Consider yourself invited, Connor. I'll let you know the details later."

He narrowed his eyes. "What the hell are you talking about, Andie? I'm the one who's getting married, not you."

"Oh, didn't I tell you? I've decided to marry Alain after all."

Slowly Conn got to his feet, feeling the blood starting to thrum in his temples. "Quit fooling around, Andie. Enough's enough. I know you're just trying to—"

Her eyes glittered with anger. "I'm not *trying* to do anything, Connor. I'm going to marry Alain. I've already called him and told him I'll be in Montreal tomorrow."

"You called him?" Something went through Conn like a sword blade, ice-cold and deadly and right through the heart. He forgot to breathe for a moment or two, his mind wheeling with the enormity, the impossibility, of what she'd just said. "You actually told Alain DeRocher you're going to marry him?"

"Do you have a problem with that?"

Somehow, Conn managed a bark of laughter, raking his hair back with his hand. "A problem? A *problem?* Good God Almighty, woman, of course I have a *problem* with that!" His voice reverberated through the room and he fought to lower it, trying to stay calm. "You don't love the man! How the hell can you marry him when you don't even love him?"

"Oh, so now marrying someone you don't love is a problem." She just looked across the desk at him, her eyes as cold as ice. "My God, you are a piece of work! You'd do it, wouldn't you? Marry Olivia and expect me to just step into the background and pretend it doesn't matter."

She gave a rough, unsteady laugh, shaking her head slowly. "No more, Connor. I've been through this more times than I can count already. Sharon Newcombe. Liza. Judith. And all the others, all your in-between girlfriends. Well, no more. Good old Andie isn't taking it anymore. I am out of here. You're on your own."

"I don't know what the hell you're talking about!" It was a bellow of anger and confusion, and he glowered across the desk at her, wanting something that made some sense.

Something softened in her eyes for just a moment, a hint of gentleness that warmed her mouth. "I know you don't, Conn. And I guess that's the real reason I'm leaving."

He simply stood there as she turned and walked out, not really believing it. Still not believing it as he watched her walk through the outer door to her office a few minutes later without even a backward glance, closing it quietly behind her.

He took a deep breath. Then another. It was very quiet. Too quiet. As though all the energy and life had been drained from the world. He could hear the old antique clock on the wall behind him ticking. Could hear, faintly, the sound of traffic on the street below. Voices, far away. Unimportant. The sound of his own heart beating, echoing in the emptiness his life had just become.

He felt oddly hollow. As though he were merely a shell of someone he'd once been, the core of him gone, nothing left but the outer wrappings. He thought, fleetingly, of the Becktron deal. Of how hard it was going to be without her.

Without her.

It wasn't possible, of course. She'd get halfway home and realize she'd overreacted and would be back up here, a bit embarrassed, laughing about it. And it would be like old times again. Just him and Andie against the world.

It made him feel better, thinking it through like that. He sat down and started reading the production report she'd found for him, but none of it made much sense. Margie came in, her eyes red-rimmed, not looking at him, putting some things on his desk and walking out again without a word. He heard the elevator whisper to a stop down at the end of the corridor a little while later and looked up expectantly, waiting for Andie to come striding through the door, hair flying, eyes sparkling, trailing laughter and sunshine and that special magic she always had.

But no one came through, and after a while he told himself he was being stupid and to get back to work. She'd be back. She had to come back. She was his best friend. And best friends didn't just leave like that.

But she didn't come back. And he went home that night more pensive than usual. He thought of calling her three or four times but decided not to, half-afraid of making things worse until he could figure out what had gone wrong.

He was still thinking about it when he went to bed a little after midnight. Lay awake half the night thinking about it, dozing once or twice then jolting himself awake, calling her name.

And finally, just before dawn, he made up his mind. He'd call her and tell her he was coming over. That they had to talk it out. Work it out. That she didn't have to marry DeRocher. That she *couldn't* marry deRocher. Because she didn't love DeRocher, she loved him.

I guess because I love you, you idiot. I always have....

Conn felt something cold run through him, hardly breathing, the words echoing and reechoing through him. *Because I love you.*

She hadn't just been saying the words because they were what he'd wanted to hear at that moment. She'd meant them.

Andrea Spencer was in love with him. *I always have.*

"Oh my God." A wave of vertigo washed over him and he closed his eyes. Love. The one damn thing in this entire universe he didn't understand.

It had always eluded him. He'd thought at one time that love and passion were the same thing. That if you had the heat, you'd have the fire. But Liza had proved that wrong. And Judith. He'd stirred up considerable heat with both of them, but it had died out. Not even embers remained.

With Andie, it was different. There had been moments of passion—with enough heat to set the world aflame—but with her, there had been something else, something deep and profound and *important.* Something he'd never really taken apart and looked at until now. A quiet thing. A solid, never-ending thing.

Love.

Slowly, very slowly, he eased out a tight breath he hadn't even known he'd been holding. Thought of it again, letting the word run through him.

Montreal. She was heading to Montreal to marry Alain DeRocher.

Swearing breathlessly, he was out of bed in the next heartbeat. Not even bothering to shower or shave, he pulled on his clothes and grabbed his car keys and was out the door in under ten minutes, heart hammering against his ribs.

She would still be there, he told himself with forced calm as he wheeled out of the driveway. She hadn't left yet. He wouldn't be too late.

* * *

If she could just stop crying, damn it, everything would be fine.

Andie gritted her teeth and battled against a fresh flood of tears, refusing to give in. Poor Alain. He was looking frazzled and harried and worried half to death, and his mother obviously figured her future daughter-in-law was a nut case.

Even the staff in the huge château had started looking at her a little oddly. She knew they were whispering about her in the back corridors, rolling their eyes in that expressive Gallic way when they saw her starting to puddle up again for no reason.

Just thinking about it brought tears to her eyes and she fought them gamely. Two days. She'd been here with Alain and his mother for two days, and they had next to nothing accomplished.

There was so much to do. The invitations. The catering. The church. The reception. Plane tickets to buy for her family. Plans to make for the honeymoon.

The honeymoon. Fresh tears welled up and spilled, and she swallowed hard, dabbing at her nose with a tissue. This had to stop. She had to get a grip on herself. She had a wedding to plan. A life to plan.

Alain was talking about kids already, and they hadn't even chosen the menu for the wedding reception. James, he'd told her this morning. He wanted to name their first son James. It made her laugh for some reason, thinking of her with a son named James. Thinking of herself married.

Flowers. Damn, she still had to choose the flowers. . . .

Getting to Montreal had been the easy part. He'd stood in Sea-Tac airport and had calmly told the ticket agent that if he didn't get on the first plane headed east, he would purposefully and calmly start taking the place apart.

But there had been a screwup in Denver, connecting flights that didn't connect. He'd gotten himself rerouted to

Dallas, then to Atlanta, then to Chicago, missing the critical flight out of O'Hare by ten minutes. There had been a choice: wait until morning and go straight through to Montreal, or cut across to New York, catch a commuter to Toronto, backtrack to Montreal.

He'd done it finally, only to find that DeRocher and his bride-to-be were at the estate somewhere outside Quebec City.

Bride-to-be. The word gnawed through him as he swung the big import through a series of curves on the winding road that led—he hoped—to the DeRocher place. At least he hadn't been too late. There was still time.

If he could find the damn place. He glanced at the rough map the kid at the last gas station had drawn for him, trying to read it and stay on the road, wondering if he should have turned left back at that last crossroad.

Bride-to-be.

If he could find the place. If he wasn't too late.

"Roses, of course." Alain's mother said it slowly and clearly, as though Andie weren't really comprehending. "White and pink. And lilies. Just a simple bouquet is so effective, don't you agree?"

"Absolutely," Andie said with a bright smile, not having a clue what she'd just agreed to.

"And we must settle on the wine for the reception. Alain does have a wonderful cellar here, of course, so that shouldn't be a problem. Oh, and we *must* decide once and for all on the dessert course."

"Triple-Threat Chocolate Surprise," Andie said wistfully.

"Triple *what?*" Alain's mother looked at her strangely. "Never heard of it. Sounds frightfully rich. I'll see if Cook can find the recipe." She gave a sniff. "I was thinking of *Crème brûlée.*"

"Whatever." Andie swallowed a sigh, looking longingly at the door. She wished she had the courage to simply get up and walk out. Some fresh air would be nice. But she had a wedding to plan.

"*Crème brûlée* will be fine, Mrs. DeRocher."

Snapdragons.

Conn looked at the bedraggled bouquet in his fist and cursed himself. Why the hell he'd given in to the whim to buy the things in the first place was beyond him. She'd take one look at them and kick him out for the fool he was.

If he ever got in.

He looked at the door in front of him and took a deep breath. It looked about a foot thick, as though someone thought it might have to hold out marauding armies. But it was by God not going to hold him out. Lifting his fist, he pounded on it again.

It whipped open and a tall, broad-shouldered woman glared at him, asking something in rapid-fire French. When he shook his head, she said, in heavily accented English, "You must go to the back. All people to help with the garden, to the back!"

"I'm not—" He caught the door just as it was slamming closed, planting himself firmly in the way. "I want to see Andie Spencer."

"Andie? Spencer?" She made the names sound exotic and foreign. "*Non, non. C'est impossible.* Go to back door. Gardeners to back door."

Conn drew in a deep breath to argue with her, then just stepped by her. "To hell with it," he muttered, ignoring her angry protests. Striding down a center hallway the size of a football stadium and trailing an increasingly wrathful contingent of distraught servants, he bellowed Andie's name a time or two, deciding he'd wasted enough time.

"Pâté de foie gras, of course," Alain's mother was saying, frowning over the written list in her hand. "Lamb. Pheasant. Venison."

"*Venison?*" Andie snapped back into consciousness. "You want me to eat Bambi at my own wedding?"

Alain's mother blinked. "Bambi? Why, my dear, we—"

"Andie! Damn it to hell, Andie, I know you're here! *Andie!*"

The voice bellowed up from downstairs like a battle cry, and Andie went utterly motionless. Now she was hearing things, she decided calmly. She looked at Alain's mother, hoping she hadn't noticed anything.

But she'd heard something, too. She stared at Andie for a horrified moment, then got to her feet. "What on *earth*—"

And then, suddenly, he was there. Connor, all six-foot-one of him, wide-shouldered and thunderous, filling the room with noise and energy. Three servants tumbled in after him, all talking at the top of their voices, all falling instantly silent at the sight of Mrs. DeRocher.

The silence stretched taut. Conn stared across the room at Andie, and she just sat there, staring back at him in astonishment. He looked terrible, his clothes wrinkled, hair in disarray, face heavily stubbled. It looked as though he hadn't changed his clothing or shaved in days. And he was holding a bunch of snapdragons, she realized numbly. He'd always known she loved snapdragons.

"And who," Alain's mother asked regally, "are you?"

"Connor Devlin, ma'am. And I'm here to take Andie home."

"Home?" The elegant voice rose slightly with indulgent amusement. "I think, young man, that you are in the wrong house. Or certainly in the wrong century."

"What are you *doing* here?" Andie's voice was just a furious whisper.

"Taking you home," he repeated stubbornly.

"You can't just come in here and—" Andie caught herself. Drew in a deep breath. "Connor, please leave. Now."

"No damn way." To her astonishment, he grinned, shaking his head in that slow, deliberate way he had. "You're mine. And I'm taking you back to Seattle. Now."

"Have you lost your mind?"

"Young man, I think—"

"Excuse me." Very gently Conn grasped Alain's mother by the elbow and escorted her to the door, shooing servants ahead of him like a flock of geese. Then, even more gently, he closed the door on the lot of them.

Andie opened her mouth, then closed it again, not having the faintest idea of what to say. He'd lost his mind, obviously. Maybe he was having the same kind of premarital meltdown that she was.

He looked at the flowers in his left hand for a moment, then handed them to her. She took them automatically.

"Andrea, I don't even know where to start."

Andrea? She looked at him more closely. She couldn't remember him *ever* calling her Andrea. He really was in bad shape.

"Conn, would you like to sit down?" she asked gently. "How about a cup of coffee?" She gestured toward the silver carafe on the low table by the fireplace. "A drink?"

"I don't want to sit down, I don't want coffee, I don't want a drink. I want you." Slowly, as though half-afraid she'd bolt if he made a sudden move, he walked toward her. "You were right the other day when you said I couldn't see what was right in front of me. But it took damn near losing you to realize I love you. Probably always have."

"You love me." She said it dryly, trying not to laugh. "Is this your idea of a joke, Devlin? Because it's not going to work. I am not coming back to work for you. Alain and I are getting married in four days, and—"

"I love you."

He said it almost defiantly this time, jaw jutting forward slightly, as though daring her to deny it. Andie just looked at him, her mind a sudden blank.

"Well, damn it, aren't you going to say something?" He raked his hair back, looking exasperated and impatient, and started to pace. "I just didn't recognize it, that's all. I always figured love was...hell, *passion*. Fireworks. Hand grenades. I didn't know it felt like a warm blanket. I didn't know that what I've been feeling about you all this time was *love*."

"Conn…" She had to stop, finding it difficult to breath. "Conn," she repeated softly, "is this some sort of revenge thing? Are you telling me this now to get even with me for—"

"No, Andie." He walked across and put both hands on her shoulders, looking down into her eyes, serious and suddenly very calm. "I know you're in love with me. I *know* that. What I'm trying to explain is that I'm in love with you. Not just that I *love* you, but I'm *in love with you*. There's a difference."

"I know." She tried to laugh, but it came out a sob.

"I don't want you to marry Alain DeRocher, I want you to marry me. I want you to come back to Seattle and marry me and live with me. I want you in my life, Andie. Forever."

"Blood brothers?" Her voice broke slightly and she gazed up at him, hardly even daring to believe.

"Husband and wife." He settled his mouth over hers, kissing her lightly. Evocatively.

The door behind them burst open, and Conn wheeled around, putting himself squarely between Andie and whoever was coming through.

Alain DeRocher stood there for a moment, eyes blazing. Then he gave a snort of laughter. "So it is you, Devlin. My mother thinks one of the gardeners broke in to kidnap my fiancée."

"I am," Conn said bluntly.

Alain nodded, a smile playing around his mouth. He was taller than Conn remembered. And heavier through the chest. If push came to shove—literally—it would be a close call.

"I wondered if you'd get here in time." The smile widened. "I was getting a little worried actually. If you hadn't turned up, I didn't know what the hell I was going to do. Marry Andie and keep my mouth shut, or do the honorable thing and come out to Seattle to pound some sense into that thick skull of yours.''

Andie gave a whuff of indignation and stepped around Conn. "What do you mean, you didn't know what you'd do? I thought you loved me!''

"I do," DeRocher said gently. "Problem is, sweetheart, you don't love me.''

"I most certainly do!''

Conn nearly grinned. She sounded almost normal again.

"You love Devlin, not me. I've always known it, but I sort of hoped...well, it doesn't matter now." Smiling, DeRocher walked across and held out his hand. "You're a hell of a lucky man, Devlin. I just hope you know *how* lucky. Because if you screw up and hurt her, I'll—''

"I'm not going to screw up." Conn took DeRocher's hand and shook it firmly. "Not this time. This time it's love. And this time it's forever." He looked down at Andie, who was still staring at him as though not quite believing he was real. "Let's go home.''

Eleven

Andie stood for a thoughtful moment at the top of the companionway leading down to the head. Then she turned and tottered back to where Conn was stretched out on the teak deck of the anchored sailboat, watching her in mild concern.

"Are you going to be all right?"

"False alarm." She was still looking a little pale, though, and she sat down beside him with a thump.

"Damn it, Andie, if I'd known you were going to get seasick, I'd never have suggested this trip. You never used to get sick when we went sailing."

"I'm not seasick. I'm pregnant. There's a difference. Although at the moment I couldn't tell you what it is."

Conn had to laugh, reaching out to slip his fingers around hers. The twin bands of gold and diamonds on her ring finger caught the sun and glittered, and he ran his thumb over them wonderingly. Four months married, and he still

couldn't believe it. And this time, he had no doubts at all
that it was for keeps.

Andie tipped her face up to the sun and he smiled again,
seeing that some of the color had come back into her cheeks.
This being pregnant routine wasn't that easy to get used to,
either. Three months already. Six to go, and he'd be holding his first child.

"We still haven't come up with an idea for a wedding gift
for Margie and Frank." Andie spilled suntan oil on her fingers and started smoothing it along her arm and shoulder.
"They're getting married in a week. I can't believe it."

"I can't believe I nearly let you get away from me," Conn
said quietly. "I can't believe I didn't see it. That I didn't
know." He subdued a shudder, thinking of what his life
could have been like if he hadn't gone after her.

She'd be married to DeRocher now. And him? Hell, he'd
probably be married to Liv Woodruff, and halfway to his
third divorce.

Andie smiled and reached down to unknot the beach
towel she'd wrapped around her earlier. It dropped to her
waist and she put her arms over her head and stretched like
a cat, bare breasts already fuller with pregnancy. "I can't
believe you nearly let me get away, either. I'd pretty much
given up on you, and that's the truth."

"Do you think that's a good idea?"

"I won't stay out long enough to burn."

"I wasn't talking about the sun. I was talking about me."
Grinning, he rolled over and lifted up onto one elbow to
nuzzle one sun-warmed breast, touching the nipple with his
tongue and smiling as he felt it grow hard. "You're giving
me all sorts of ideas here, lady."

"Good ones?" Her voice was filled with laughter and she
cradled his head against her.

"Damn right." He slid his hand between her inner thighs
and pushed them apart gently, knowing she wasn't wearing
a thing under the towel but suntan. They'd made love a

scant hour ago, but he was aroused and hard already, wondering if he'd ever get his fill of her. Doubting it.

"Connor..." Laughing, she lay back languidly. "What *are* you up to?"

"No damn good," he murmured, kissing the delicate, soft skin on the inside of her thigh. "I think your mother warned you about men like me."

"Numerous times." Her breath caught. Caught again.

Smiling, Conn traced a leisurely line of kisses up the soft swell of her belly and across her left breast, pausing there for an enjoyable moment or two. Then, finally, he found her mouth with his and kissed her even more leisurely.

And wondered, as he wrapped his arms around her, how he had ever thought that love was a complicated thing.

Love was looking down into his wife's eyes and seeing everything he ever needed to know. Love was waking in the night and watching her sleep beside him, her mouth still touched by laughter, and knowing it was forever. Love was the tight, warm hug he felt around his heart every time he even thought of her.

Love was . . . his best friend. Forever. And always.

* * * * *

Cruel Legacy

One man's untimely death deprives a wife of her husband, robs a man of his job and offers someone else the chance of a lifetime...

Suicide — the only way out for Andrew Ryecart, facing crippling debt. An end to his troubles, but for those he leaves behind the problems are just beginning, as the repercussions of this most desperate of acts reach out and touch the lives of six different people — changing them forever.

Special large-format paperback edition

OCTOBER
£8.99

W🌐RLDWIDE

▼ SILHOUETTE *Desire*

COMING NEXT MONTH

FAMILY FEUD
Barbara Boswell

Man of the Month

Shelby thought her blue blood couldn't mix with Garrett's blue-collar background. But Garrett vowed that before long he'd be teaching her about mergers and acquisitions...of the most intimate kind!

THE UNFORGIVING BRIDE
Joan Johnston

Children of Hawk's Way

Falcon Whitelaw had vowed never to get married. So why was he saying 'I do' to widowed mother Mara—a woman who hated his guts?

LEMON
Lass Small

Brown Brothers

Lemon Covington hated fortune-hunting females who wanted big rings on their fingers. Then he met Renata—but she wouldn't bother to notice him. So what could this confirmed bachelor do?

SILHOUETTE

Desire

COMING NEXT MONTH

MEGAN'S MIRACLE
Karen Leabo

Megan was flabbergasted when Holt Ramsey claimed she was the natural mother of his adopted son! But why was there something hauntingly familiar about the boy?

OUTBACK NIGHTS
Emilie Richards

Russet Ames thought she was on her way to a new life in Australia. But she hadn't counted on old family friend Daniel Marlin meeting her at the airport…

UNDER THE BOARDWALK
Carla Cassidy

Greyson Blakemore was back—and he wouldn't let Nikki forget about the fiery kisses they'd once shared. But Nikki had vowed never to let him back into her life…

COMING NEXT MONTH FROM

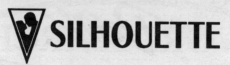 SILHOUETTE

Sensation

A thrilling mix of passion, adventure and drama

SECRET FIRES Kristin James
COLD, COLD HEART Ann Williams
KIDNAPPED! Kate Carlton
WICKED SECRETS Justine Davis

Intrigue

Danger, deception and desire— new from Silhouette...

SQUARING ACCOUNTS Patricia Rosemoor
CUTTING EDGE Caroline Burnes
DÉJÀ VU Laura Pender
CACHE POOR Margaret St. George

Special Edition

Satisfying romances packed with emotion

THE PARSON'S WAITING Sherryl Woods
A HOME FOR THE HUNTER Christine Rimmer
RANCHER'S HEAVEN Robin Elliott
A RIVER TO CROSS Laurie Paige
MIRACLE CHILD Kayla Daniels
FAMILY CONNECTIONS Judith Yates

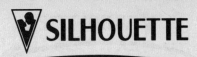

WORDSEARCH

Win a year's supply of
Silhouette Special Editions
ABSOLUTELY FREE!

Yes, you can win a whole year's supply of
Silhouette Special Editions. It's easy, just
find the hidden words in the grid below!

SPECIAL

MYSTERY

EDITION

TEDDY

SILHOUETTE

GIFT

S	L	O	V	E	A	Z	H	G	S
G	I	E	D	I	T	I	O	N	U
O	I	L	W	B	O	O	K	T	E
O	S	F	H	C	P	S	I	E	C
D	P	L	T	O	W	F	S	D	N
K	E	G	R	X	U	R	S	D	A
I	C	M	Y	S	T	E	R	Y	M
Z	I	A	N	A	R	D	T	K	O
T	A	N	Q	U	I	D	I	T	R
P	L	E	B	J	M	Y	L	S	E

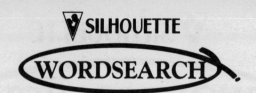

SILHOUETTE

WORDSEARCH

The first five correct entries out of the bag after the closing date will win one year's supply of Silhouette Special Editions (six books every month for twelve months). Worth over £100! **What could be easier?**

Don't forget to enter your name and address in the space below then put this page in an envelope and post it today (you don't need a stamp). Competition closes 30th June 1995.

SILHOUETTE WORDSEARCH
HARLEQUIN MILLS & BOON,
FREEPOST,
PO BOX 344,
CROYDON CR9 9EL.

- ✂ - - -

COMP195

Are you a Reader Service subscriber Yes ☐ No ☐

Ms/Mrs/Miss/Mr _____

Address _____

_____

_____ Postcode _____